BURMA FILE

Dale Dye

"Dale Dye uses words to paint a cinematic landscape. Shake Davis, a larger-than-life character, also possesses a realistic humanity and compassion that is incredibly relatable. It is an incredible read."
— Keifer Sutherland, Actor, *24*

"Shake Davis is back! Author Dale Dye gives us action, guts, and a fitting Memorial Day tribute to the glory of our warrior's past. A gripping tale of pride and commitment to the courageous values that made America great."
—Mark Greaney, #1 *NYT* bestselling author of *One Minute Out*

"Locked and loaded with action and mayhem: oh-man does Shake Davis deliver! From stem-to-stern…filled with all the guts and twice the glory. Read it today!"
—Rip Rawlings, bestselling author of *Red Metal*

"Dale Dye proves himself once again to be as good a storyteller as he was a soldier during his own distinguished military career, bringing his stalwart Shake Davis back to the grounds that define him to this day on a Conrad-esque journey into the heart of darkness….Dye manages to combine the pacing and plotting of Stephen Hunter with the angst-rattled soldier's sensibility of Phillip Caputo. He hits the bulls-eye dead center, resulting in a tale as riveting as it is relentless and not to be missed."
—Jon Land, *USA Today* bestselling author of the Caitlin Strong series

Also by Dale Dye

DELTA FILE
BANGKOK FILE
SEA HUNT
AZTEC FILE
HAVANA FILE
CONTRA FILE
BEIRUT FILE
CHOSIN FILE
PELELIU FILE
LAOS FILE
RUN BETWEEN THE RAINDROPS
PLATOON
OUTRAGE
CONDUCT UNBECOMING
DUTY AND DISHONOR

BURMA FILE

DALE DYE

WARRIORS PUBLISHING GROUP
LOCKHART, TEXAS

BURMA FILE

A Warriors Publishing Group book/published by arrangement with the author

PRINTING HISTORY
Warriors Publishing Group edition/May 2023
All rights reserved.
Copyright © 2023 by Dale A. Dye
Cover art copyright © 2023 by Gerry Kissell

ISBN: 978-1-944353-45-2
Library of Congress Control Number: 2023938159

The name "Warriors Publishing Group" and the logo
are trademarks belonging to Warriors Publishing Group

PRINTED IN THE UNITED STATES OF AMERICA

10 9 8 7 6 5 4 3 2 1

To all of you over the years—in and out of
uniform—who kept my personal creek unmuddied
and allowed the creative juices to flow. So many. So
little space. But you know who you are. Thank you.

Lockhart, Texas

I t was over at 0545. He left the bedside where he'd been parked through the night and walked out onto the widow's walk where they'd spent early hours watching so many flamingo-pink tangerine-orange Texas sunrises. One of those uniquely colorful dawns was just breaking, but there was no joy in this one, no sense of a new beginning. There was only grief, a sense that life as he'd come to know and love it was ended.

She'd gone quietly. No fuss and drama to it. Just a slow halt to her breathing. He didn't bother to call to Dr. Wheeler, who was puttering around with the coffee maker in the kitchen downstairs. The doc said it was imminent. She was right. Just as she'd been accurate in predicting that this was likely to be Chan's last day after six long months of battling an aggressive and lethal cancer. Chan had personally made all the arrangements in meticulous detail during that time. Arrangements would shift to autopilot soon as Shake made the first call on her list.

He'd tried to lend a hand with the planning at first, but it was so depressing that he'd eventually left it to her. And while she phoned around town or talked to friends and relatives, he walked to the shady spot on the property where just two months earlier they'd dealt with another tragic loss. She'd wanted something simpler for the big dog's gravesite, but he'd insisted their beloved Bear be memorialized like a fallen soldier with a miniature rifle he'd carved stuck in the ground and bearing the set of dog tags he'd had made for him.

The doctor silently padded by him on the way up as Shake Davis descended the stairs. In a day or two, the old house would be crowded with friends and mourners remembering the life and times of Chan Dwyer Davis. But for at least a few minutes on this day, her husband wanted to physically be as alone as he felt. He walked down the slope toward the creek and collapsed under the tall pecan tree that shaded Bear's grave. He'd seen death in all its forms over a lifetime of service in and out of uniform and learned to deal with it. Inside him somewhere was a sort of mental cave, a private little Golgotha where the rock was only rolled away when he allowed it. But this was different. There was no hiding from this pain, no stiff upper lip, none of the continue-the-march stoicism he'd always used to mask his emotions. He reached out and laid a hand on the big dog's marker.

"She's gone, boy. And I think maybe I am too."

Moei River, Thailand/Myanmar Border Region

They found the old man clinging to a mossy log, afloat but barely alive. Two fishermen, seining for perch where the river ran wide and deep north of the town, hauled the wizened elder into their boat and motored for the refugee camp to the south. He was in rough shape, dehydrated with running sores on his arms and legs. And not all the damage had been done by the jungle. It looked to them as if the old man had been severely beaten, probably with bamboo canes, likely the handwork of the Tatmadaw, Myanmar's corrupt military. Or perhaps one of the bandit gangs that waged constant battles for turf and cross-border drug smuggling routes. They didn't need to question the man and he could not have answered if they did. The only question that needed an immediate answer was whether he would live long enough to reach medical help.

He was hardly the first refugee that they'd encountered and helped to escape a brutal subsistence across the river in Myanmar. The fishermen didn't understand the politics involved but they knew desperation when they saw it and they'd seen plenty of it among the wounded, sick and brutalized people who flocked to the riverbanks to escape into Thailand. The way of the Buddha emphasized compassion and the fishermen could see from the amulet on a leather cord around the old man's scrawny neck that he was a follower of the path. If he lived, the old man would join thousands of others all along the border who lived homeless and hopeless lives depending on the tender mercies of various aid organizations.

A delivery truck driver they flagged down on the road leading south to Mae Sot gave them a ride to the teeming camp and his rescuers carried the old man, flopping between them like a deboned perch, toward a large clapboard structure marked with a red cross. Chesa Ngo rushed to help when the patient was carried in for treatment. As soon as she had cleaned up some of the filth on his face and body, she recognized the old man. He was from her village, an elder and close friend of her father's. When Chesa was a teenager, and her sister Endra was just a baby, the old man would enchant them for hours, telling stories about trips to famous *stupas* and educating the girls about Nat spirits that lived in the jungle.

"He's a tough old bird." The doctor on duty, a jaded realist volunteer from Australia, finished his initial examination and prescribed a rehydration regimen plus broad-spectrum antibiotic treatment. "Bit of a waste given his age, but I reckon we should do what we can after what he's been through. I'll look in on him tomorrow…if he survives the night."

Chesa was left to clean and treat the wounds, scrapes, cuts, and abrasions that covered the old man's body. She silently prayed for him to live so that she could get some news of her family. It had been nearly two years since she spoke with her sister, an unexpected international call on a borrowed cell phone. Since then, Chesa heard nothing but worrisome reports of continued violence by roving bandit gangs and brutal raids by the Tatmadaw attempting to stamp them out of Karen tribal territories. Other refugees reported that her village was lately unmolested. But it's Myanmar. And that means it is only a matter of time.

Chesa Ngo, a registered nurse working for the Thai-Burma Border Consortium, spent the rest of the day recalling myths of her childhood, asking the old man's Nat spirits to intercede in his recovery. She knew it was silly, but she felt better for doing it. After dinner she called her husband, who was in Bangkok on a business errand, to tell him about the old man and her hopes that he'd have information about her family when he was recovered enough to speak. Walter was skeptical and cautioned her once again about getting overly involved in problems she could not solve.

And then she went down to the river the Thai's called *Moei* and her people knew as *Thaung Yi*. The jungle was dark and impenetrable along this stretch of the water. She knew from her childhood that the jungle hid all sorts of dangers. Lots of jungle predators these days were human. She ached to get her family out of Myanmar. His parents would probably refuse. They were old fashioned, hard-headed, and yet remained optimistic that things would get better in their native lands. Her sister was another story. Endra deserved a chance like her older sister got years ago.

She understood that what she and others were doing for refugees here in Thailand was not nearly enough and likely would never be unless the situation in Myanmar's tribal lands changed radically. Her husband and others poured money into the effort, but that largess barely covered necessities for the flood of people who crossed the border every day. Here at Mae Sot, Walter's generosity kept Thai or Burmese staff paid, but they mostly did maintenance or other scut jobs. Any necessary medical procedures—and there were plenty of those every day among the refugees—had to be performed by a handful of qualified doctors or nurses on staff at Mae Sot. And there were never enough of those, most of them here on short-term volunteer assignments.

It was often makeshift cut-and-paste medicine, constantly short of everything but sick or injured patients, but the refugees in this camp were mostly her people. Chesa was a Karen, the only one she knew that managed to escape village life. And there was a lot of blind luck involved in that, some of it due to international aid organizations who recognized an exceptional child. Or missionaries who funded her opportunities when they came.

And Chesa counted herself lucky to have met Walter Ngo when she was studying in America. Walter was Vietnamese born and had an abiding interest in his native land, even if it was only economic these days. He became a very rich and successful man over the years. There was not much he could do personally for the citizens of his native country, so Walter threw money at it. He was a businessman first and only a grudging part-time philanthropist, so he made huge investments in Vietnam through his Lancer Technologies empire which produced videogames and other consumer technologies with native Vietnamese labor and skill.

Myanmar was a different story and a much more personal one for Chesa. Her people needed more than jobs or a boost to the national economy. They needed help just to survive, to escape the brutality and corruption that tainted life for everyone in Myanmar outside a small circle of tycoons and tyrants in Yangon. And that would take more than her time and Walter's money.

It was two days before the old man was recovered enough to speak. Chesa was smiling brightly when she brought him soup and tea, anxious to pump him for information. He began to weep as soon as she sat down beside his cot. "My girl, my little girl," he groaned with tears streaming down his face. "You must be brave. The news from our home is terrible..."

Chesa sat quietly as the old man told his story, her stomach churning and her throat constricted, trying to hold back her own tears. About a week ago—the old man wasn't sure about date and times—a band of cutthroats had surrounded the village. They were looking for young women to kidnap and sell to brokers who procured Bamar women to work in Thailand's brothels and bars. Endra, now a beautiful and blossoming teenager, and three other young village women were prime targets. Chesa's parents tried to fight back to protect Endra. It was the last act of parental courage they performed. A bandit killed them both with his machete. No one else in the village was willing to challenge the fate of the kidnaped women after that. The bandits took the women along with anything else they fancied. The old man followed for a day, looking for a way to rescue the village women. Perhaps he would find a Tatmadaw or police unit that he could trust. But he saw no one in authority while following the bandits. They caught him stalking their camp one night and beat him severely, leaving him for dead when they departed heading for the Thai border at dawn. There was some more mumbling, mostly about how the old man made his way to the river and rescue, but Chesa barely heard any of that.

When she couldn't bear any more, she sat and sobbed silently. The old man tried to comfort her with talk of karma and fate, but Chesa Ngo had lived too long among Americans who believed fate was something that could be adjusted, altered, or avoided with a lot of effort and a little luck. Her mother and father were gone, the old man had seen them hacked to death with his own eyes, but Endra was probably still alive. She was too valuable for the bandits to sacrifice. That gave Chesa some hope and a goal. She started working on it immediately. She called Walter in Bangkok and told him the story and her plan to cross into Myanmar and pick up her sister's trail. If she hurried and brought along a few of the tough men available in the Mae Sot camp, she might be able to rescue Endra before her sister was sold into a sordid existence that would ruin her life.

Walter Ngo was adamant and forbid her to cross the border. As soon as he wrapped up his affairs in Bangkok, he promised to fly to Yangon and spend whatever was necessary to mount an official search. He'd get the authorities on the case no matter what it cost. That was a good plan for Walter who still believed in things like law, order, and justice. Walter didn't understand that sex trafficking was so pervasive in many areas of Myanmar, that the authorities tended to ignore it, especially if there was profit in it for them—and there usually was.

He didn't know what his wife knew about the brutal sex trade. He didn't frequent the Thai bars, clubs, and brothels filled with exploited Burmese women who had no future beyond the next trick or the next dose of drugs that kept many of them chained beyond any hope of a normal life. Walter's money wouldn't buy much more than platitudes and promises in Yangon. If Endra was to be saved, it required quick and effective action.

Chesa had some personal cash, funds she squirrelled away for certain things she needed or wanted without having to ask Walter. That bought her three guides from among a raft of ready volunteers at Mae Sot. She'd picked what she thought were the most capable of the lot. Two because they were former Tatmadaw soldiers and had guns hidden in the jungle. One because he had a semi-reliable truck and claimed he knew most of the trafficker's routes from personal experience.

They'd been on a series of rutted, overgrown back roads for just two days when the ambush hit them near the Irrawaddy River. Two of her escorts were killed without ever firing a shot from their weapons. The third man disappeared into the jungle chased by bandits. She was spared mainly because she was sleeping in the bed of the truck when the bandits struck. And because they quickly discovered they had another female for the auction block.

A one-eyed man seemed to be the leader of the bandits. She heard him called Pak by several of the men who all seemed to have some sort of military organization. He took Chesa Ngo's cell phone and passport before his men shoved her away from the crippled truck and marched her along a jungle path that led to a rough bamboo enclosure. There were five captive women inside the rickety enclosure, all starving and half-naked.

One of them was Chesa's sister.

Lockhart, Texas

So how long?" Mike Stokey skipped a stone across the surface of the creek that bisected the property. Three jumps. He'd gotten better at it over a week of trying—mostly failing—to pull Shake up from the depths of a very dark depression.

"How long what?" Shake ran a five-inch panatela under his nose and inhaled, trying not to light one of his favorite cigars. It was one of the last in his humidor. She'd almost made him quit. Didn't matter much now. He flipped open his Kershaw and sliced an end off the smoke.

"How long until you get up off your ass and do something with the rest of your life?" Maybe a bit harsh, but Mike was running out of soft soap and Shake had always responded best to straight talk anyway. "I know how bad you're hurting, Shake, and that's the way it goes when you lose someone you love and who loves you the way she did." Mike took the lighter out of his friend's shaky hand and ran the flame over the end of the cigar. "She's gone, Shake, and you're not. Simple as that."

Shake puffed the panatela into a bright glow and exhaled fragrant smoke into a soft Texas breeze blowing across the creek. "Two things, Mike. They keep it from being simple as that."

Mike turned to study the lines and angles in Shake's craggy face. The gallons of whisky they'd consumed over the past week would alter anyone's visage, but this was something way beyond the ravages of a long bender. The contour lines in that facial map he knew so well were dangerously steep.

"Well, we're sober enough to be serious right now, so run it down for me."

"Thing one…my give-a-shit gauge is pegged on empty. And thing two…even if 1 found something—anything at all—that I cared about, I don't think I've got enough juice left to handle it. I'm empty, Mike…Winchester…out of ammo."

Three hours later, full of Black's BBQ brisket and half a bottle of TX bourbon, Shake fell asleep on the couch. Mike Stokey pulled out his mobile phone and rummaged for the business card in his wallet as he walked out onto the screened porch. The neatly embossed card bore the logo of Lancer Video Technologies on the front, but Mike was interested in the private mobile phone number scribbled on the reverse. The man who gave Mike the card in Las Vegas had been looking to contact Shake, anxious to hire him for a special job in Southeast Asia. A couple of day later, before Mike felt comfortable in broaching the subject, Chan died. Then just wasn't the time. Now maybe it was.

Walter Ngo, President and CEO of Lancer Video Technologies, answered on the second ring. "Mike! Recognized your number. Did you talk to him about it?"

"Not yet, Walt. Timing just didn't seem right. He's hurting…pretty bad. His wife just died."

"Oh, hell. I'm really sorry to hear that. Hard to imagine life goes on when something like that happens. But it does."

There was a long uncomfortable silence on both ends of the call. "So…" Walt Ngo finally broke it. "What kind of shape is he in? Will he see me?"

"He needs something, Walt. Shake needs something to focus on beside what he's lost."

"Mike, listen—if I could just get a couple of hours face time. I really need a man like Shake right now. The situation I'm facing is turning desperate."

Stokey thought it over and decided it was worth a shot. Whatever Walt Ngo's problem was, it might just be something a man like Shake Davis would be anxious to help solve. Anything that gave his friend a new focus was worth a try. "OK. Head for Austin. Let me know your flight details and I'll pick you up at the airport. No promises, Walt, but I'll get him to listen. That's all I can promise."

Walter Ngo punched off the call and hit the speed dial to alert the crew of the Lancer corporate jet, a Gulfstream 650. Flight plan for south central Texas. Ten a.m. departure from Vegas Harry Reid to Austin-Bergstrom and RON.

He'd play hell explaining the expense to his Board of Directors. The bastards were trying to edge him out, but that was a fight he'd have to delay despite skating on some very thin corporate ice. He had a more pressing personal problem, a problem that he simply couldn't handle by himself.

Ngo retrieved his laptop and reviewed the research material he'd had compiled on the man he was to meet in Texas. No question the guy had a heroic war record, a ton of experience in Southeast Asia, plus a nearly unbelievable post-military record of accomplishing difficult things against very long odds. And he was interested in an interview he found that said the old warhorse had a romantic streak, well-read in classic literature. Shake Davis was the kind of man he needed.

He packed an overnight bag and then pulled up his personal finance pages. It was ugly and getting worse, but he needed fluidity. He was hedging assets, selling off and hiding cash like some kind of artful tax dodger. If he lost control of Lancer he'd be in a serious financial bind. And rescuing his wife was likely to be a costly endeavor.

ဏ

"I'm most definitely not in the mood, Mike." Shake blew steam off the top of his coffee cup and watched a kettle of red-tailed hawks gliding through a bright blue morning sky.

"Call it a favor for me, Shake." Stokey scooted a lawn chair into a patch of shade thrown by one of the towering live oaks in the front yard. "Just listen to what the guy has to say."

"Who the hell is he again?"

"Walter Ngo. N-G-O which you should recognize as a Vietnamese family name. Out of Sacramento originally where he founded a highly successful tech outfit. Made a mint in systems and videogames. One of the golden boys in the geek world. Everything he touches turns to gold."

"How do you come to know some honcho in an outfit like that?"

"Got a call from Ron Keene. Remember him? Former Marine FBI Guy in Vegas. He was in Nam with us…late war. Keene tells me he got a call from this gazillionaire who operates out of Vegas and the guy is looking to get in touch with Shake Davis. Keene gives me a number and I called just to let the guy know it was bad timing for you."

"Should have just told him to fuck off…"

"I tried but Walt Ngo's pretty persistent. He keeps pressing. Guy's got an interesting story, so I let him talk. He's Vietnamese, originally from our old stomping grounds around Danang. His folks were killed when he was just a baby, and he got passed through a Catholic orphanage until Operation Babylift in '75. He winds up Stateside and gets adopted by a family in Las Vegas. High school, college at UNV. He did about six years in the Army, got out, started this tech company called Lancer Video Technology and bang-zoom, he's a multi-millionaire."

"What's he want with me?"

"He's got a problem in Myanmar, what used to be Burma. I didn't get any details, but it's apparently serious. He'll run it all down for you when he gets in." Mike checked his watch. "I'm picking him up in a couple of hours. Anyway, just listen to the man. I think you'll be interested in what he's got to say."

"I'm not…"

"Not what?"

"Not interested…" Shake simply shrugged and stared into his coffee cup.

"Well, goddammit, I'm interested in you hearing him out! Can you do that for me? For Christ's sake, just listen to the man!"

"OK…so, I'll listen." Shake glanced at his watch and then headed for the house.

"Where are you going?"

"Liquor store. Said I'd listen. Didn't say I'd listen sober."

ၵ၇

Shake was tolerant but not very attentive as they sat on the screened back porch around a butcherblock table on which a full bottle of bourbon formed the centerpiece. The host of this hasty meeting seemed mostly interested in a crimson-plumed cardinal perched on a nearby oak limb. On the other side of the table, Walter Ngo, the recently arrived guest, was laser focused.

"Mr. Davis, for the past couple of years, my wife and I have been trying to help with the refugee situation along the Burma-Thailand border. She's Burmese, originally from the Karen tribe, a trained nurse, lovely woman with a huge heart. I was mostly just there to write checks and do whatever else I could."

Shake nodded and splashed Old Granddad into their glasses. "Make it Shake from now on." And then he turned his attention back to the bird now preening vivid red feathers.

"My wife is missing, Shake." Ngo inhaled whisky fumes and took a swallow. "We were over there two weeks ago working in a camp at Mae Sot on the Thai side when my wife got a report that her family had been killed in a rebel raid. Chesa was a wreck—and the news from the interior just made things worse. Reportedly, her younger sister, a teenager she adores, had survived and was on the run for the Thai border. Chesa demanded I hire some local guns and mount an expedition into Burma looking for her sister."

"Instant and very expensive rip-off," Shake mumbled.

"That's exactly what the people in the border camps told me, but family roots run deep over there. Locals kept telling us that most likely her sister was either dead or in the hands of some people who would sell her off into forced labor. Chesa wouldn't hear it. She's a very stubborn and determined woman."

Ngo sat forward with his elbows on the table. "Mostly to keep her calm, I left Chesa at Mae Sot and flew to Yangon to appeal for some official help." He hit his whisky and exhaled. "That's where I blew it. While I was in Yangon, another refugee showed up at the camp, a guy Chesa knew. He tells her that sister Endra was captured with some other women by an outfit that specializes in human trafficking. By the time I got back to Mae Sot, Chesa was gone. Crossed the border with a couple of locals to go rescue her sister." Ngo smacked a hand on the tabletop. "Goddammit! I warned her to sit tight and let me work it, but she wouldn't listen!"

"Tough situation…" Shake was studying Walt Ngo's expression carefully now. He understood the pain the man must be feeling. He was feeling it himself. "I understand what it's like…" He stopped and hit his whisky glass.

There was an uneasy silence as Walt Ngo studied the man across the table. He felt like a sleazy salesman trying to up-sell a vulnerable mark.

"I was heartbroken…sure you can understand. The way things are over there, she could very well be dead. And then one of the guides she hired showed up at Mae Sot. Said they'd been waylaid by the same outfit that had Endra. Nasty bunch of bastards affiliated with the Karen National Progressive Party. The guy said when he left Chesa and her sister were alive, moving east along the Irrawaddy River.

"That means they're probably headed for the Thai border. And that means they intend to sell off the women. It's SOP. They get big bucks for females who end up as sex slaves or worse."

"No help from any official sources?"

Ngo sat back and crossed his arms. "I tried to pull strings at the State Department. Got a lot of talk and indignation but no action. Even if the U.S. bureaucrats got off their asses it might be too late."

"And no luck with the Burmese?"

"The Burmese government—or what passes for a government in Yangon—is too concerned with the Rohingya genocide situation to pay much attention to anything else."

Mike sipped his whiskey and tried to recall what he knew about the Rohingya in Myanmar. "Those are Burmese

Muslims, right? And the government is trying to shoehorn them out of the country?"

"Yeah. It's the government's biggest headache right now. Nobody wants Muslims in a Buddhist country, I guess. They're driving them into exile in Bangladesh, which isn't happy about the situation either. Lots of international outrage, so the government in Yangon has no time for anything else. Chesa and her sister are just another couple of missing women among thousands all over the country."

"Why aren't you over there trying to rescue your wife instead of sitting here telling us about it?" The way Shake said it, the question seemed more like an accusation.

"That's where I want to be…but I just can't do it that way. I need a guy like you to do it for me."

"Why?"

"It has to do with who I am and what I do…"

"That's gonna take a little explaining."

"If the people who have Chesa find out she's my wife, they'll be demanding a huge ransom. That's one thing and I could deal with it. But if I go after her personally, if they captured me, it's a whole different ballgame."

"Again…why?"

"I'm the face of one of the biggest videogame producers in the world, Shake. Tons of money involved. I've been all over the internet ads for games. I'm even featured in the intro to a couple of our most popular releases. And even Burmese kids play lots of videogames."

Mike Stokey nodded. "So, if you cross into Burma looking for her and get nabbed, they've got a huge cash cow in hand."

"That's about the size of it." Ngo shrugged. There was more to it, but Walter Ngo didn't want to muddy the waters with his business problems. "It's just not something I can risk trying to handle on my own."

"Lots of ex-snake eaters over in Thailand who might take on a mission like that."

"These traffickers are thugs, Shake. Long on guns and short on brains. I can't just hire a bunch of cowboys who might start a shooting war and risk getting Chesa and her sister in the middle of a firefight. I need a man like you…"

Shake twisted the cork back into the whiskey bottle and exhaled, tapping a forefinger on the table. "Shit, man—even if I was willing to give it a try—you've got to know what a long-shot something like that would be."

"My whole life has been a series of long-shots, Shake. I believe they can pay off, given the right man and proper motivation."

Shake Davis sat quietly thinking. He'd survived some serious long-shot odds over a lengthy career doing dangerous things in both war and peace. He was motivated one stupid way or another back then. Now, he wasn't at all sure he was the right man with any sort of motivation to go on living at all. On the other hand, he thought eyeing the capped whisky bottle, if it was his time to buy the big dirt farm, maybe better to do it on some kind of useful mission, even if it didn't stand much chance of succeeding. He'd seen too many men he admired drink themselves to death when the frantic pace of their lives suddenly slowed to a listless crawl. Or they couldn't get over losing someone they loved.

Walter Ngo had triumphed in business because he knew how to exploit opportunities, spot a rival's weaknesses. He sensed he might have a shot at getting what he needed from Shake Davis with just one more little shove. He was prepared to throw a lot of money—money that he really didn't have—at a rescue mission, but it was delicate for a lot of reasons. He needed a man who was motivated by something other than money.

"You ever been to Burma?"

Shake looked up, a little startled by the question. "Got close a couple of times…Thailand, Laos, Vietnam, all over most of the Golden Triangle, but I missed Burma somehow."

"Fascinating place, fascinating people. All very exotic and alluring. My wife just seemed to personify all that to me. Perfect mixture of that exotic beauty and hard-headed survival instincts. Lots different than what I remember about my people in Vietnam. Maybe the contrast is what drew me to her in the first place, I don't know. But I love her a lot and I want her back safe, out of that mess over there."

"Always promised my wife we'd visit Burma." Shake looked at his empty glass and shoved it away from him. "She is…was…half Thai. Pissed her off when I'd start quoting Kipling."

"By the old Moulmein Pagoda," Ngo recited quietly. "Lookin' lazy at the sea, there's a Burma girl a-sittin' and I know she thinks of me…"

"On the road to Mandalay…Shake nodded. "…where the flying fishes play. And the sun comes up like thunder out of China across the bay."

"Come you back, you British soldier." Walt Ngo finished for them. "Come you back to Mandalay."

༺༻

Mike Stokey found Shake smoking a cigar by the creek later that night. He was fairly sure his friend had decided to give the Burma job a shot after hearing him on the phone with his daughter earlier. Tracy Davis, discharged from the Navy Reserve, was looking for a quiet place to work on her latest oceanography research paper, and her dad was offering the big house in Texas as a refuge. Shake wouldn't have made the call if he wasn't needing someone to watch the place while he was away.

"You're thinking about it, right?"

"Kind of…on a tangent really."

Stokey used a flashlight to illuminate the giant bullfrogs that croaked along the far bank. Their eyes flashed like jewels when the light hit them, but Shake didn't seem to notice.

"What's that mean?"

"Just means I was thinking of Burma but in another context." Shake sucked on the cigar and flopped down next to his friend. "I was remembering a guy I met one time at a VFW thing up in Austin…survivor of Merrill's Marauders, one of only a handful left these days. The dude had some wild stories about service in the China-Burma-India Theater during World War II, especially about fighting in Burma."

"Don't hear much about those guys in the CBI, do you?" Stokey was hoping there was another attraction to the proposed Burma mission swirling around in Shake's head. He was intimately familiar with his friend's hobby of exploring esoteric battlefields around the world. A trip with him to one of these out-of-the-way places was akin to a graduate level course in military history.

"Ass-end of the fight against the Japanese…" Shake watched the sparking arc of the cigar butt he tossed into the creek. "Japs were in control of most of Southeast Asia by around 1944. Holding a very thin allied line were a few British and Indian Army outfits. In Burma the best fighting unit was British General Orde Wingate's Chindits. Vinegar Joe Stillwell was there, but his command was the Chinese Expeditionary Force, and it was questionable at best. Vinegar Joe wanted an American infantry outfit operating under

American command that could go deep through the jungle and hit the Japanese in their own territory. He pulled up a hard-ass brigadier named Frank Merrill."

"Hence Merrill's Marauders, I'm guessing."

"Affirmative. Merrill cobbled together a unit made up from stateside volunteers and some GIs who had jungle fighting experience in the island campaigns to carry out long-range raids and deep-penetration missions against the Japs in Burma. On the books it was the 5307th Composite Unit—parentheses—Provisional. Very tough, very light and very long-suffering outfit that quickly became known as Merrill's Marauders."

"Speaking as a guy who has some lengthy experience with jungle fighting…" Stokey chuckled remembering his three back-to-back tours in Vietnam. "I'd say those poor bastards had a very tough row to hoe."

"Understates the case," Shake mumbled. He had multiple tours in Vietnam himself plus some serious training and operations in jungles around the world, but he'd always heard that Burma was a whole different thing, one of Asia's most formidable environments. "Always had this idea about walking that ground, you know? Seeing what Merrill's Marauders saw and getting a little better idea of what they faced during the war."

"Well, Shake. Here's your chance. If nothing else, you could write a hell of a book when you get back home."

"Maybe…" Shake levered himself up, patted Bear's grave marker and headed for the house. He wouldn't write a book. Likely he wouldn't make it back home anyway. And that was just fine.

Burma Jungle, east of the Irrawaddy River

Chesa Ngo was exhausted and dazed. Her sister Endra was weary but better off at 15 and used to a hardscrabble village life. But that wasn't saying much. Both women were nearly naked, sitting along a barely visible jungle trail, in what rags were left of their clothing. Their bare arms and legs were scraped, scratched, and covered with insect bites.

For the past three days, they'd labored along through dense jungle, heading east if Chesa's estimate of direction based on the sun was accurate. She fully expected the rebels to head for the Thai border, but they'd avoid the teeming refugee camps that dotted the area. Chesa had interviewed enough Burmese women in those camps to know the drill. If things ran to course, the ten rebels, led by one-eyed Pak, would take them to some remote border area where they'd be auctioned off into Thailand and forced labor or prostitution. So far, they'd been unmolested beyond a few pats and pinches, but that couldn't last.

But today turned out to be different. Four of the six female captives were culled from the group and sent off into the jungle with three rebels escorting them. Chesa didn't know why the other women in the group were sent away, and none of the remaining guards answered her questions beyond laughing and grabbing at their crotches. There were just the two of them held captive now in this little jungle clearing near the river. And she had to protect her sister.

Chesa pulled a small vial of ointment from her first-aid kit, the only possession she retained after the violent encounter with the rebels that killed two of the three men she'd hired to take her on the search for Endra. She told the rebels she was a nurse and promised to help with wounds or sickness if they let her keep the little bag of bandages and medicine.

Her American passport and cellphone were now in Pak's kitbag. Given the violence and surprise of the encounter in the jungle, she'd had no chance to call her husband, but he'd be looking for her. He was likely angry that she'd disobeyed and crossed the border. It was a bad idea, but there was nothing to do about that now. Walter would rescue her. He was a man of means and connections. She just had to survive and keep Endra safe until then.

She dabbed some disinfectant onto her sister's legs and buttoned up the girl's shirt. The tattered garment came from a rebel's pack when Endra's own native blouse had literally rotted off her shoulders along the trail. Endra insisted on keeping it unbuttoned claiming it was too hot otherwise, but the flash of her budding breasts was causing some of the rebels to grab and fondle.

As a rural teenager having no experience with intimacy, Endra tended to laugh off the encounters as innocent boy-girl flirtations. Chesa warned her constantly, but the scolding didn't help much. Endra was careless, and Chesa thought she was secretly enjoying her status as a sex symbol. She had only the vaguest notions about men and their carnal appetites.

The Karen rebels who had them were cruel and ruthless. She'd seen that in the initial encounter with them. From the uniform remnants most of them wore and the weapons they carried, Chesa thought the rebels were former Tatmadaw soldiers, maybe deserters. Beyond that, she knew nothing about them or their intentions.

While the rebels gobbled a meal of rice and jungle fruit, Chesa walked off into the bush to empty her bladder. Squatting with her cargo trousers around her knees, she looked up to see one-eyed Pak grinning at her, leaning on a mangrove tree and talking on a cell phone. He was a tall, willowy man with a snake-skin patch over his left eye. A long jagged scar extended from his hairline to his left cheek, likely a souvenir of the encounter that cost him the eye. So far, the rebel leader had been aloof: approachable but never prone to casual conversation or answering her questions.

She stood, buttoned up, and walked toward him. He stuck the cell phone in his pocket and pulled out her American passport. "You are not just a nurse working with the refugees," he said paging through the passport. "I think you are much more than that, Miss Chesa. Buddha smiles. You are a lucky one."

Before she could question him, Pak turned and shouted at his men to get moving. They had a new destination, he said. They were moving west to Moulmein. Chesa had no idea why the change in direction as she helped Endra to her feet and followed the rebel column through the jungle. She prayed that it might have something to do with her husband and efforts to free them.

Over the Pacific

He spent most of the long flight from LAX to Danang scrolling on his laptop, reading background material that Walt Ngo sent immediately after Shake agreed to undertake the reconnaissance or rescue mission…whatever it turned out to be. And Ngo apparently meant what he said about sparing no expense to get Shake on mission in Southeast Asia. He was booked first class across the Pacific to Vietnam, then Bangkok, and finally Yangon.

There was plenty of room and minimal airline distractions on the Thai Airways International flight. Shake was able to spread out and study maps and what seemed like a metric ton of background material on the country. It was all interesting, might even prove valuable at some point during his mission, but the foreign affairs eggheads consistently referred to Myanmar and Yangon. Shake found it distracting—probably down to age and Rudyard Kipling's influence—so he just trained himself to mentally substitute Burma and Rangoon as he read through the material.

Burma was a major battlefield in the fight with the Japanese during World War II. After the war, the country remained a British possession until it was granted independence in 1948. That was a new deal for the Burmese. The country was always tribal, and nobody knew squat about central governance. The result was the longest ongoing civil war in the modern world. Hot and cold running juntas in Rangoon. A few weak passes at democratic elections, but the military always was and still is the power in the country. And the Burmese military was shot through with corrupt leaders who could give a shit less about what happened in the countryside as long as they got rich and hung on to power.

Couple rampant corruption with no effective internal law enforcement plus the ongoing tribal conflicts and you've got lucrative territory for drug smugglers, human traffickers, and all sorts of other illicit activities run by strongarm cartels in Southeast Asia. The Burmese people are caught in the middle, mostly just trying to survive. And that creates a massive refugee situation along the country's borders.

Shake yawned and rubbed his tired eyes. He skimmed a slew of bureaucratic stuff from area experts on government, ethnic composition, and military infrastructure, but he lingered a long time over a pithy document written by a military attaché in Rangoon. Apparently, Ngo had somehow filched it from classified State Department files. The author was a Marine Major likely doing an obligatory joint-service, cross-over tour and clearly not thrilled with an assignment out of the Fleet Marine Forces. Shake didn't recognize the name, but he was betting Major Sherman Semple was a fellow mustang officer. The man wrote like a grunt. He called bullshit freely and frequently when he saw it, using plain, forceful language potent enough to send diplomats into dithering flaps.

The Marine Attaché pointed fingers and named names about corruption in the Burmese military, money-grubbing border guards, the ongoing tribal warfare, and the plethora of "little piss-ant guerilla groups" that were selling violent services to drug-smugglers and human traffickers all over the country.

And that explained why the document was classified. Shake mentally marked Major Semple's paper as gospel from a straight-shooter and filed it for further study. When he finally reached Burma one of his first stops would be a visit to Major Sherman Semple at the American Embassy.

Unfortunately for Shake's vaguely planned scheme of operations, reaching Rangoon as a rolling point in the search for Mrs. Chesa Ngo and her sister was going to take a few days, maybe as much as a week—longer than he'd planned. Seems a guy can't just fly into Burma, stock up on supplies, and head out into the tribal lands, which was about as far as his current level of planning extended. There was a guy in Danang, director of Walt Ngo's major software production facility in Vietnam, who would provide area business credentials covering Shake as a Lancer Tech researcher on a field assignment. And then there was another guy in Bangkok, also a Lancer Tech executive, who would provide any updated information from Karen tribal lands and hand over a large bundle of cash for use in greasing Burmese palms where and when required once he reached the area he was determined to search. Beyond those contacts, Shake understood he'd be pretty much on his own looking for some slippery outfit called the Karen National Progressive Party. Or more likely some offshoot guerilla force doing the KNP's dirty work, assuming Walt Ngo's wife and her sister were still with them and not already dead or sold off to some pimp gathering girls for work as hookers in Bangkok.

It was a daunting mission full of pitfalls and boobytraps, not well-planned or thought-out the way something this difficult should be. *Like trying to pick fly-shit out of a pile of pepper,* Shake thought as he fell asleep somewhere over the Pacific. He found himself wondering if Chan would have wanted him to do something so likely to fail or get him killed deep in a Burmese jungle. It was some small comfort to Shake that he believed she would.

Danang

As the aircraft taxied off the active runway, a lilting announcement in three languages welcomed passengers to the Democratic Republic of Vietnam. Everyone seemed anxious to disembark after 17 hours crammed into a jet-propelled aluminum tube, but the jostling crowd was held back to let the first-class passengers go first.

Shake stuffed his research material into an envelope, tucked his laptop under an arm, and descended the airstairs onto the tarmac. A sign above the terminal entrance proclaimed he'd reached Danang, but Shake didn't need that affirmation. As he entered the building and walked toward passport control, he could have been blindfolded and it wouldn't matter. He was back in the Land of the Lotus Eaters. The babble of sing-song voices and the fishy smell of the muggy atmosphere oriented him immediately. It looked a lot different superficially, but every sense told him he'd returned to the place that had been his old base of operations for nearly three years a half-decade earlier.

He felt a minor adrenaline jolt as he approached a bored bureaucrat who flicked a hand toward Shake's extended passport. The man was uniformed in familiar olive green festooned with red collar tabs. The last place Shake had been face-to-face with a Vietnamese in a uniform like that was in Hue City during the Tet Offensive in 1968. And those guys were brandishing AKs instead of the rubber stamp the immigration official slammed down on his passport. The Vietnamese cop favored his American visitor with a belch that reeked of *nuoc mam* and waved him through to the baggage claim area.

As Shake waited for his old jungle rucksack to emerge onto the carousel, his cell phone pinged a text alert. It was from Nguyen Than, his designated Lancer Tech contact, politely apologizing for business that prevented him from meeting his guest personally. The text told Shake to take a taxi to the Orchids Hotel in downtown Danang. Mr. Than would meet him for dinner at 1900.

The first cab in the rank outside the terminal roared up immediately as Shake emerged from the terminal and a driver with a mouthful of gold-capped teeth motioned for him to climb in the back of a rusty Citroen powered by an engine that wheezed and belched painfully from a diet of cheap gasoline. Shake told him his destination, but the driver hesitated. "You pay pee or dollah?" Shake waved a twenty in green which was promptly snatched as his driver ground a cranky transmission into gear for the trip downtown.

Shake sat back on the rump-sprung bench seat and tried to focus on his upcoming meeting with Nguyen Than. He needed some kind of information that would enable him to pass as an employee of a high-tech development outfit, but what a guy like that would be doing in Burma was beyond him. Hopefully, Than would provide answers and enough background to help build a credible legend. He was bound to be bumping into military patrols or internal security cops where he was headed. His map study coupled with Ngo's information indicated he'd need to search a large strip of land west of the Thai border in the Karen State. It was the last known location of the rebels who had Mrs. Ngo and her sister in captivity. And it was one hell of a lot of jungle.

Hopefully, there would be some more specific information available from the Lancer Tech contact in Bangkok.

And then on to Rangoon with a pocket full of money that Walt Ngo warned him would be crucial to passage all along the way. According to Ngo, there were very few encounters with military or government authorities in the countryside that could not be sidestepped with an appropriate application of cash. Shake was skeptical, but Ngo assured him that there was no place in the hard-scrabble Burmese countryside where a visitor could not find some military or police official willing to be bribed.

Shake was trying to arrange all the warnings, cautions, and advice into some sort of short-term plan during the ride to the hotel, but it was hard to concentrate. The cab dodged like a berserk bumper car through snarls of four-wheeled traffic flanked by swarms of motor scooters, motorcycles, and pedal bikes. The helter-skelter traffic patterns he remembered from an occasional Jeep trip through downtown Danang during the war hadn't changed that much. There were new paved roads to replace the potholed dirt streets he remembered. And the streets now featured painted lines and curbs, but no one seemed to pay them much mind.

The cabbie honked and muttered curses as he bulled the vehicle through the two-wheeled crowd blocking his right turn into the broad sprawl of Vo Nguyen Giap Boulevard. The right rear quarter of the cab swiped a Vespa ridden by a Vietnamese beauty who was steering the scooter with one hand and thumbing a text into her iPhone with the other. She peeked out from under a pink Hello Kitty helmet and growled something at the cabbie. When the cabbie responded with a longer and louder horn blast, she waved it off and rejoined the scooter throng with the skirt of her *ao dai* fluttering in the exhaust fumes.

Shake couldn't remember what the street now named for the old NVA warhorse and field commander was called during the war. Or even if it had a name back then. He just remembered that it was a broad, palm-shaded thoroughfare that led to Red Beach where his outfit occasionally staged a beer-bust and barbecue near the South China Sea. He shouldered his ruck at the Orchids Hotel entrance and looked up at the tall building's neon-lit façade. The place looked both pricey and gaudy, likely designed to appeal to Asian tourists who began flocking to Vietnam when the dust settled after the long war finally ended. From what he could see of the lobby looking through lengthy polished windows, the hotel featured the Asian minimalist style, dark wood and plentiful polished brass favored by the Chinese designers who likely built it.

A trim little doorman wrestled the pack off Shake's shoulder and elbowed him toward the lobby entrance. Shake offered his passport to a raven-haired beauty wearing a pristine *ao dai* and a polished brass nametag that identified her as Miss Song. She bowed, smiled, and began to click away on a keyboard. With his identity and reservation confirmed somewhere on a hidden computer screen, Miss Song handed over a keycard for the door to Suite 401 plus a pile of handouts touting various hotel services and shops. A bellman in livery that made him look like the front-rank trombone man from a college marching band plunked Shake's musty old pack on a baggage cart and headed for the elevators.

As Shake moved to follow, Miss Song interrupted, waving a pink message form. "You have dinner reservation," she said in passable English. "Mister Tran. Seven p.m." Miss Song's delicate features scrunched into a frown. She seemed to be worrying about something she wanted to add. "He to meet you in…" She pointed toward a long hallway lined with fragrant tropical plants in polished brass pots.

"Crissanamum Restaurant!" Miss Song smiled happily. "Very good food."

Shake glanced in the direction indicated and saw a purple neon sign indicating the entrance to the Chrysanthemum Restaurant. Nodding his understanding, he followed the bellman. On the ride up to his floor Shake glanced at the brochure for the restaurant. Fusion cuisine with Vietnamese specialty dishes and a four-star rating from the South China Morning Post.

The bellman opened the door to the suite and Shake followed him inside wondering through a fog of jet lag why the hotel owners wouldn't call their four-star eatery something poor Miss Song could pronounce. The bellman was delighted with the greenback single Shake offered and left him alone looking down through a plate glass window on the busy late afternoon traffic thronging the streets of downtown Danang. Close your eyes, ignore the scents of sandalwood and tropical flowers, and you could be standing in some stateside Hyatt or Hilton with the air conditioning dialed down to meat-locker levels. He had about four hours before he was to meet Nguyen Than for a briefing that would likely require a clear head, so he decided on a long shower and a short nap.

♾

Feeling somewhat more refreshed after two hours of sound sleep, Shake stood at the marble-topped bar adjacent to the restaurant sipping the first of only two beers he'd decided to allow himself during the short stay in Vietnam. His system was still reeling from all the bourbon he'd poured down after Chan died, and he recognized that a whiskey taste and a boatload of grief could become a deadly combination. He needed to discipline himself, but it seemed like everything he saw or sensed in Vietnam reminded him of his wife in one way or another. He was hungrily eyeing the long line of liquor bottles behind the bar when a dapper little man in a muted business suit approached with one hand extended and a shrink-wrapped package tucked under an elbow.

"Mr. Davis," the man said in precise English with only a hint of Vietnamese lilt, "I'm Nguyen Than." Shake accepted an embossed business card, pocketed it, and shook the man's hand. "I am regional manager for Lancer Technologies here in Vietnam." The bartender approached with a deference that said Than was a regular and respected customer. When Than waved a hand, the barman scurried away to mix his regular drink. It turned out to be Johnny Walker, Blue Label served neat. Than relished the whiskey for a moment and then raised a cut crystal glass.

"Welcome to Vietnam. I regret you won't have much time here. Mr. Ngo has booked you on a six a.m. flight to Bangkok departing tomorrow morning."

"Well," Shake responded with his raised beer bottle, "Mr. Ngo is paying the freight and giving the orders, so whatever you say is fine."

"Since time is short, I suggest we discuss our business over dinner?" Than downed his drink and motioned toward the dining room. They followed a receptionist to a curtained booth at the back of the room where Than ordered another drink and waved away the proffered menu. "I took the liberty of ordering for us," he said. "I think you will like my selection. Local prawns done in a very fine Vietnamese sauce. A little spicy for some. He pointed at Shake's local beer. "But delicious with cold beer."

"I'm a little surprised," Shake said when a fresh beer arrived at the table. "I didn't know a company that makes videogames would have a branch in Vietnam."

Than hit his drink and chuckled. "It often surprises our investors and customers, but many such games are designed and manufactured in Asia. Most of Lancer's top-selling games were developed right here in Vietnam. We have a talented staff of designers, artists, and programmers. They are top shelf in what is known as first-person shooter video games."

Shake thought that one over. First-person shooter style videogames were among the most bloody and violent on the market. He'd heard a lot of bitching about their supposed influence on a young generation of addicted gamers, but he had no idea that Asian geeks had such a big hand in the business. Maybe it had something to do with the violent history of this part of the world.

"And that brings me to our business tonight." Than handed over a bulging manila envelope and paused while their dinner was served. When the main course was between them on the table, Than ignored the polished silver and used his fingers to dive right into a platter of sizzling shrimp.

"That package contains complete background on our operations here in Vietnam, Thailand, Singapore, Hong Kong, and a few other locations in Asia. It should bring you up to speed on our design and manufacturing process." Shake put the envelope on the bench seat next to him and tasted the prawns. Than was right. They were thick, juicy, and delicious with a bite that demanded a cold beer chaser.

"So, I guess I'm supposed to be on some sort of research assignment in Burma?"

"Yes. You are credentialed as a designer doing research for a new video game which Lancer Technologies is anxious to produce. The player is a member of U.S. forces fighting the Japanese during World War II. We have several very popular games on the market involving the war in Europe. This is to be our first production designed around the war in this part of the world. The paperwork I gave you has more specific details."

"And the Burmese—or Myanmar-ese or whatever— would welcome something like that?" Shake grinned, thinking about a videogame where the player was a Chindit or a Merrill's Marauder. Might even buy one of those myself. If I could find a kid patient enough to teach me how to play it.

"Oh, yes…" Than dunked a shrimp into a silver sauce bowl and munched. "While the average Burmese probably doesn't know much about what happened in their country during the war, they are very aware of videogame game culture. We sell a lot of games in Myanmar, Mr. Davis."

"And that's my pitch? I'm working on something that would be a big hit in Burma."

"In Burma and lots of other places around the world where videogames are popular. And that's practically everywhere these days. You are in the country photographing and collecting detail of the Myanmar jungles so our artists can recreate them for the game. I expect you will find everyone most accommodating."

Than wiped grease off his fingers and reached for the package he'd carried into the restaurant. "This is a Nikon D3200 digital camera with an 18 to 55 millimeter zoom lens. Very fast shutter speeds. Very good for low-light situations."

"I don't know much about photography," Shake said as he examined the little black camera that Than pulled from the box.

"That's the marvel of today's technology," Than said tapping a finger on the camera's instruction booklet. "You don't need to know much more than point and shoot with a camera like this. No film. Everything is saved on a chip." He hit his drink and went after more shrimp. "And who knows? We might actually produce such a game one of these days."

After dinner, Than left Shake with a caution to be early for the morning flight to Bangkok. Back in his suite, Shake paged through the background material on Lancer Technology's Asian operations. Apparently, once a concept for a videogame was established, approved, and funded at the corporate level, local video geeks in parts of Asia got hot and designed the background, characters, and action according to a detailed script. Then the whole thing was forwarded someplace else for tweaks and testing before it went stateside, where Lancer Tech hucksters rolled it out for throngs of gamers hungry for vicarious thrills.

Mostly skimming the included business details and corporate aggrandizement, Shake decided his legend would not require much more than convincing curious officials that he was out to capture real images of Burmese jungles and authentic atmosphere for Lancer artists and designers. He knew enough about the Chindits and Marauders during World War II to make him sound like a student of the subject—which he was anyway.

He tucked away the corporate material and picked up the camera manual. It seemed as straightforward as Than indicated. The camera contained a light meter and automatically set the shutter aperture unless the photographer overrode it. After that it seemed pretty much as advertised. Point and shoot. Point at what and shoot what didn't really matter much anyway.

Shake had just about decided to take the Nikon out for a test run, snapping a few shots of Danang for practice, when his high-tech cell phone demanded attention. Walt Ngo had provided the instrument which was set up for max international service and reception. As far as Shake knew, Ngo was the only one who had the number.

"How did the meeting with Than go?"

"Fine, I guess. Good dinner. And he gave me a camera. I'm trying to learn how to use it right now."

"Everything else satisfactory?"

"I'll know more about it once I meet with your guy in Bangkok. Any news from that source?"

"Yes. It appears the people who took Chesa, the so-called Karen National Progressive Party, have discovered who she is. They sent a ransom demand through some contacts in one of the border camps near Mae Sot."

"How'd they find out?"

"Who knows? I raised so much hell trying to get official help, the word probably filtered out to the KNP. Jungle drums or something like that."

"Well, I guess that means she's still alive. And likely to remain that way assuming you pay their price."

"Yes—and at least we know where they are. They sent instructions for a meeting. Chris Anthony, our guy in Bangkok has details. He's an old friend and fraternity brother as well as my good right-hand man in Asia."

"If you don't mind the question, what are they asking for?"

"A sizable chunk of money—which is not the problem. And some other things—which are most definitely a problem."

"What do they want?"

"Guns, weapons, explosives…a whole laundry list of stuff I can't possibly get. And I couldn't deliver things like that into Myanmar even if I could get them."

Shake thought he could see where this was going. "Before you even ask, Walt. I can't get that kind of stuff either. And frankly, I didn't sign on to become an international arms smuggler."

"I wouldn't ask you to do something like that, Shake."

"OK…so what do you want me to do?"

"Just go ahead with the itinerary for now. Given what I'm hearing from over there, I think the demand for weapons is just a test. They're trying to see how far I might go to get Chesa back. They've got to know I can't deliver a boatload of weaponry into Myanmar. I believe it's a bargaining chip, you know? They demand something I can't deliver and use that to drive up the ransom price."

"Which is what?"

"One million in U.S. dollars. And the bastards even demanded it in nothing larger than a twenty."

"Smart. From what I've seen over here, anything larger than a twenty in green in nonnegotiable. Probably something to do with the underground money swap or something."

"Yeah. These bastards are smart."

"Well, it's sure a bunch of money…" Shake thought about some of the claims for massive profits and investment capitol that he'd read about in the Lancer Tech background material. Given the big bucks claimed to be available for research and development, a million seemed like chump change. "Lancer should be able to pony up that much, right?"

"Doesn't work that way, Shake. I answer to a board of directors in the company. I can't use corporate funds for something like this, no matter how much I'd like to."

"I guess it's really none of my business, Walt, but you must have fairly deep pockets yourself…"

"I can lay my hands on a million from personal assets, Shake. But it would take some doing to transfer that much cash in small denominations, and we'd need a pallet and a forklift to deliver it. And the security problems? Jesus Christ, we try to truck that much cash from Thailand to Burma and get through checkpoints at the border? Probably never even reach the people holding Chesa and her sister."

"Yeah. I can see the problem. You'd be dragging a big hunk of cheese through a nest of hungry rats."

"Precisely. But I think I might have a better idea."

"And it involves me?"

"It does. But I don't want to discuss it on the phone. Chris Anthony in Bangkok is working it now. He's a fraternity brother. Capable man. Meet with him and we'll talk again when you get there."

After the phone call, Shake sat wondering about the change in his mission to Burma. On the one hand, it was a lot simpler. They at least knew where Chesa Ngo was being held inside Burma. Most important to Walt Ngo and the mission in general, they now knew Chesa Ngo was still among the living. No mention of the teenage sister, but Shake thought it must be a package deal. Might be as simple as getting from Rangoon to the specified location, paying the ransom demand, and escorting the hostages across the border into Thailand. But Walter Ngo was right about the landmines involved in delivering a cash ransom. Getting a pallet of greenbacks across the border and through a stretch of guerilla-infested jungle would require something like an armored infantry battalion as escort.

And it seemed a safe bet the bad asses fronting the Karen National Progressive Party would balk at taking Walt Ngo's personal check. Shake paced the suite trying to figure out what Ngo and his Lancer exec in Bangkok were scheming to meet the ransom demand. A guerilla outfit operating deep in the Burmese jungle wasn't likely to have a bank standing by for a wire transfer. And they'd likely never heard of the standard negotiable monetary instruments used in corporate finance. Shake pictured himself confronting some sarong-wrapped squirrel brandishing an AK and asking if the man took traveler's checks.

Walt Ngo was in a bind, but he'd seemed relatively calm and collected on the call. Shake found it hard to imagine himself in the same fix. Could he stay cool if it was Chan being held in a chaotic cesspool like Burma? Likely he'd already be on the hunt, shooting his way through any and all obstacles.

Maybe a man like Walt Ngo, used to dealing in high finance and cut-throat corporate maneuvers, had learned to keep a lid on personal emotions. Maybe. Anyway, Shake could always back out if the scheme for paying the ransom demand was too ridiculous. Or maybe something ridiculous, ultra-risky, and likely to produce a wild-ass adrenaline jag, was just what he needed right now. Hard to say.

Shake pulled open the mini fridge under the work desk in his suite. As he reached for a plastic bottle of cold water, he saw a rank of one-shot whiskey bottles arrayed on a shelf. *What the hell*, he thought. *Who cares?* Shake fisted two little bottles of Jack Daniels Tennessee Sour Mash, twisted off the caps, and had his first hard drink since leaving Texas.

The whiskey went down with a satisfying bite but Shake shut the fridge on the remaining liquor. A couple of snorts was one thing. Hitting the booze hard in his current state of mind, facing so many unknowns on a half-baked rescue mission in a country he'd never before visited, was something else. He would need what focus he'd managed to muster for at least a little bit longer.

Mostly to distract himself and partly because he was wondering if he'd recognize the old Red Beach party venue,

Shake grabbed the camera, hung it around his neck, and went for a walk. The little map on one of the hotel brochures indicated he was just a short walk away from *My Khe* Beach, a place simply called Red Beach when various military units in and around Danang used it for in-country R&R seaside outings. Likely nothing of the old Seabee shelters and barbecue pits would remain, but there might be something familiar. He and his buddies from the 1st Marine Division had spent some good times taking a break from the war on that beach.

Miss Song, apparently pulling a double shift at the reception desk, pointed him toward the seashore with a smile and assurances that the beach was very nice at night. Shake pushed through the revolving door and onto Vo Nguyen Giap Boulevard. It was nearing eleven and pitch dark except for the haloed glow on the occasional streetlight but the downtown boulevards were still crowded with two-wheel motorists. He remembered that urban Vietnamese tended to save errands for after sundown when the heat was less oppressive.

Most of the passing bikes carried at least two and sometimes as many as four riders. Mom, Dad, and a passel of kids if a family was headed for a late outing or appointment. Some of the bikes were used as transport or delivery vehicles, so overloaded with crates, baskets, or produce that the driver was barely visible.

Poor folks trying to do more with less. That much about Vietnam hadn't changed. Years ago, when U.S. soldiers and Marines wandered the streets of Danang, they had to be on the lookout for Saigon Cowboys, two-cycle dirt-bike marauders who were said to be able to snatch a wristwatch off a GIs arm without ever slowing down. There were a few shifty-looking duos roaring past him as he reached the sandy strip of beach, but none of them gave Shake much beyond a curious glance.

My Khe Beach was still a popular spot even at this late hour. Teenagers in tank tops and rolled-up trousers scampered in and out of the rollers washing the sand. And romancing couples in western clothes lined a gaudy pedestrian walkway designed to look like an undulating, humpbacked dragon breathing neon fire into the night sky. Further out beyond the surf line, local fishermen in round, rickety little basket boats tended lines, trying to hook a seafood dinner. The lights hung on the rim of the boats bobbed and winked as Shake walked further down the beach, snapping the occasional picture with his new camera.

In the near distance, the familiar hump of Monkey Mountain was visible, and Shake remembered visiting an American forces radio and TV station up there once upon a time 50 years ago. The place was infamous for rampaging hordes of rock apes.

In the far distance, out beyond the horizon, on what the U.S. Navy used to call Dixie Station, there was always a flotilla of American warships waiting to intercept enemy supply convoys or provide naval gunfire support for outfits in contact ashore. Nothing even close to that tonight. This stretch of the South China Sea was placid and serene.

A chilly wind blew across the sand. The horizon was briefly lit by a flash of far-off lightning. From force of ingrained habit, Shake counted seconds until he heard a rumble of thunder. It was way out there. Probably over the horizon. He smiled remembering a ship that could fire from that far out at sea, out where a storm was brewing. Fire from that particular ship was rare in his experience, but it was always welcome, usually accurate and truly impressive.

Shake squatted in the sand remembering an operation in the fall of 1968 when he'd been supported by the biggest hammer in the Navy's toolbox, the battleship *New Jersey*. The World War II-vintage ship had lately been pulled out of the mothball fleet and sent to Vietnam. The hope was that broadsides from her massive 16-inch guns might rattle some sense into the North Vietnamese Army which was rebuilding base areas up around the DMZ.

A couple of officers from the Marine Corps Air-Naval Gunfire Liaison Company briefed the officers and NCOs from 2nd Battalion, 3rd Marines picked to spearhead the sweep of a series of identified enemy installations dotting high ground around the infamous Rockpile area north of Dong Ha. Even for combat-jaded Marines, what they had to say about "Big J" was impressive. Most of the Marines had never seen a battleship except in comic books. A few had heard tales from veteran relatives about battleships in action in the Pacific Island campaigns of World War II or off the coast of Korea in the 1950s.

Shake had been pretty certain that all of the Iowa Class battlewagons—he read somewhere there were four of them—had long since been retired. But there he sat in a leaky, smoke-clouded tent at Dong Ha, hearing about the USS New Jersey (BB-62) and plans to have her piss massive amounts of death and destruction on the NVA waiting for them up around the Z. The briefing tag-team of a Navy Lieutenant, one of the ship's gunnery officers, and a Marine Captain from ANGLICO sounded like used car salesmen touting the big ship's vitals.

"We used to have four of these big ladies in the U.S. fleet," the Navy officer crowed. "Iowa, the class ship, New Jersey, Missouri, and Wisconsin. The Big J is the only one operational today. She was launched back in 1942, before most of you were born, and then brought back to fighting trim in April of this year." There was a lot more about the New Jersey's 60,000-ton displacement, her better than 30 knot speed and her crew of 1,900 sailors, but the Marines just sat slack-jawed through that. They perked up when the Marine officer started talking about her main battery, a brace of nine 16-inch guns in three triple turrets. "Those big guns can throw shells some 23 miles, and the New Jersey will be well within that range on Dixie Station when we do the prep fires for your operation."

The Marine officer used a pointer to indicate an enlarged photo of a Volkswagen Bug he'd pinned up next to the tac map full of arrows and rectangles outlining their mission plan. "Most of you recognize the VW Beetle, right?" Nods from the audience indicated everyone was tracking. "Well, the New Jersey's sixteen-inch, .50 caliber guns fire a round that weighs nearly as much as this car." Tap, tap from the pointer. Hoots and cheers from the Marines. The consensus was voiced by a sergeant in the back row. "Fuck yeah! Get some!"

When the noise abated, the ANGLICO captain continued. "One round of HE weighs twenty-seven hundred pounds. That's more than a ton of whoop-ass for every round fired. But working with naval gunfire of this size firing from offshore, it ain't like calling in mortars or artillery and advancing under their fire. Danger close for a sixteen-incher is something like five hundred meters. That means you can sit and watch that big round fly over for a while before you have to get up and tangle assholes with the gooks."

The Navy officer concluded. "And if the Big J does her job, you might not have to tangle assholes at all."

The next morning, Shake sat with his platoon in pre-assault positions, listening to the ANGLICO radio operators talking to the ship. There was a lot more data being transmitted than he'd ever heard for a standard artillery fire mission. There was a lot of stuff about wind and weather that cannon-cockers didn't care about when they were getting ready to shoot. The Marines kept their eyes mostly glued to the mountains half a click to their front, but a few glanced backward as if they might catch sight of the Jersey's muzzle flash. They knew better. The ship was more than 20 miles away, but it was hard to resist.

And then the barrage was on. It caused everyone to flinch and reflexively duck. It was as if a fleet of screaming banshees had been loosed overhead. The big shells roared and rocketed through the air with a doppler effect that sounded like the crouching Marines were about to be overrun by a semi-truck or a speeding locomotive. It was so loud and unusual that most of them were speechless. The cheers started when the rounds began to impact on the high ground to their front. Minus the mushroom clouds, it looked to Shake like a line of mini nukes had detonated on the objective they were going to assault. He'd never experienced anything that devastating or spectacular in all his combat time.

He'd also never experienced an operation of this size in which all objectives were taken in less than four hours with only sporadic shots fired by shell-shocked enemy defenders. It was a walk in the sun for the Marines that day. The New Jersey fired 21 sixteen-inch rounds. And that was plenty. They found mostly eviscerated corpses, hair, eyes, and teeth on the objectives. And for the rest of his time in Vietnam, Shake bitched when the USS *New Jersey* was not available to fire for his unit.

Shake picked up his new camera, pointed the lens at the South China Sea, and let his imagination photo-shop in the mighty USS *New Jersey* steaming along belching flame from her primary batteries.

Maybe it was viewfinder fixation or maybe it was the double shot of Jack numbing his situational awareness, but Shake didn't notice the snarling Yamaha bearing down on him until it was nearly too late to react. And he needed to react in a hurry to dodge an imminent collision. The bike bearing two Vietnamese teenagers was roaring right at him, churning up a rooster tail of sand. As he turned to dodge, the kid on the back of the bike reached out and snatched at the camera strap around Shake's neck. That strap was new and solid. So was the backseat cowboy's grip on it. Shake was jerked off his feet into a face-plant and showered with sand from the bike's rear tire.

The bike had hardly slowed, and as he was towed behind it, Shake felt the camera strap edging up over his ears. He was determined not to lose the Nikon to a couple of Vietnamese juvenile delinquents, so he rolled hard and dug in his heels. The twin cowboys couldn't have weighed more than a buck-ten each and the camera strap was stout nylon, so Shake jerked hard against the rider's grip and pulled him off the moving bike.

Still holding onto the camera strap, the kid hit and rolled like a veteran jumper executing a parachute landing fall. A knife blade flashed in the moonlight as the cowboy slashed at the camera strap. Shake grabbed a fistful of sand and heaved it into the kid's face. While the thief pawed at his eyes, Shake scrambled upright into a close combat crouch.

Shoving the camera out of the way, he advanced watching the half-blinded man wave the blade around like some sort of berserk ninja. Amateur hour. Shake dodged a wild slash and stepped into striking distance. He spun the cowboy with one hand and used the other to deliver a hard shot to the throat just below the chin. That sent cowboy one down into the sand gagging and gasping.

It also spurred the second cowboy into action. Just as Shake was about to drive a foot into his buddy's ribs, cowboy two dumped the bike and charged. whirling a length of chain over his head in a whistling arc. Shake ducked under the arc and drove his foot into the kid's right knee. That put the man off balance but still ready to fight, so Shake improvised with the only weapon at hand.

He pulled the camera free and swung it. The sturdy little Nikon landed with a dull thud just over the man's right ear. Blood spurted and the cowboy dropped the chain to clutch at the laceration on his scalp. Shake snatched the length of chain and backed away to gain maneuver space as he motioned for the Yamaha cowboys to come on if they wanted some more.

They didn't. Convinced that they'd picked the wrong mark for their snatch and grab, the driver and his buddy stumbled back toward their bike. There was a babble of Vietnamese and pidgin English over the blat of the bike's engine as they remounted. Shake caught "sonabeech" and "muddah fuckah" but it was just angry noise. The cowboys were out of fight for the night.

A crowd was gathering nearby to watch the action out on the sand, so Shake decided to back away himself. Better flee the scene than try to explain the incident to a bunch of local cops likely being called by one or all of the observers with cell phones glued to their ears. As the cowboys wheeled the Yamaha back onto the pavement and goosed it to make their escape, Shake hurried in the other direction ducking in and out of streetlight arcs trying to look like just another tourist brushing beach sand from his snapshot camera.

If local cops were called or expressed any interest in the incident, it wasn't obvious. No flashing lights or sirens as Shake made his way back to the Orchid Hotel. He shook and stomped off what sand he could reach at the entrance and pushed his way through the revolving door. He smiled and gave Miss Song a polite wave. Then he dropped the length of greasy chain on her desk and headed for the elevators.

If his pricey new camera suffered any disabling damage in the fight, it wasn't obvious. The shutter still clicked, and the mysterious internal mechanisms still purred. The lens was still clear after he wiped off the sand residue, and there were no beeping noises or flashing alerts to indicate trouble. Shake packed it away with his other gear, showered, and hit the rack. He was hoping for a few restful hours before he had to get up at dawn for the early flight to Bangkok, but deep sleep was elusive. Maybe it was residual adrenaline from the little skirmish on the beach, but it felt like something more. Shake didn't fight it. It wasn't a jolt of rocket fuel coursing through his system, but it was a strong sensation. And somehow it felt like a welcome change.

Bangkok

"Gold?" Shake sat in the Lancer Tech conference room staring at a gilded block of metal resting on a black velvet throw. Chris Anthony, the regional manager and Walter Ngo's fraternity brother, nodded and tapped a manicured fingernail on the bold bar. "One of the world's most recognizable and readily negotiable currencies." Anthony pulled off a pair of wire-framed glasses, plucked a tissue from his pocket, and began to polish the lenses. He nodded toward a frisbee-shaped speaker resting in the center of a polished mahogany table. "It was Walt's idea. And a good one, I think, given the circumstances."

Walter Ngo chimed in on the secure line and his voice sounded just slightly tinny through the speaker. He seemed a little more stressed than the last time they'd spoken on the call in Vietnam.

"As I told you earlier, Shake, they want a million in cash plus that stupid laundry list of weapons. That's obviously a non-starter, so my idea is to up the ante with something they'll recognize as maybe more valuable than guns. They want power, status, respect, you know? Give them gold and they get all three. Nobody else in Myanmar has that kind of asset including the government. The KNP becomes instant top-dog among all the tribal groups. They'll forget the nonsense about guns and explosives. Money talks, Shake. Especially in a place like Burma."

Shake reached out gingerly and ran a finger over the gold bar. It was maybe four inches wide and ten inches long. An etched box was lettered Credit Suisse above the words *fine gold* and numbers 999.9. "I don't know what one of these is worth. But I'm betting you could buy a metric shitload of weapons with it."

"You could, indeed." Chris Anthony nodded and smiled. "The price of gold fluctuates in the worldwide market but safe to say this bar right here, right now, would bring no less than $65,000."

Shake stood, grabbed the bar, and hefted it. He guessed just under 30 pounds. He sat back down and stared at the speaker console. It was surreal. He'd always thought of this kind of thing as being buried deep in a vault at Fort Knox. Somewhere in his gear back in Texas, he had a gold watch that Mike Stokey gave him for Christmas one year. It was the most valuable thing he owned, and it wasn't even pure gold.

"So, this baby goes for sixty-five grand on a good day. That's a buck or two shy of a million. You think they'll go that cheap?"

"No. This is just a taste, enough to let them see we're serious and offering a better deal. Instead of cash and all the attendant government problems they'd have with keeping and spending it under the table, they get gold."

"And the plan is to pay the remainder of the ransom demand with more gold?"

"Right." Anthony sipped from a sports drink and leaned across the table. "While you're making the initial contact, and selling them on the concept, we assemble the remainder of the ransom price in gold and get it across the border. That presents some logistics problems, but I think I've got it handled."

"And these little guerilla dickheads squatting in the jungle are gonna know all about the price fluctuations and market prices for gold?"

"You won't be dealing with the gunmen who took Chesa and her sister, Shake. They're just local muscle. The ransom demand came from the KNP leadership, and they are surprisingly sophisticated according to what we're discovering. They're not gonna kill Chesa and her sister or sell them off to some border pimp. That's chump change. They'll be after the big bucks in solid gold."

"I can see a bunch of problems with this scheme—on your end and mine."

"It's not gonna be easy, Shake. But it will work. Trust me on that."

It was either trust Walt Ngo—and at this point Shake really wanted to—or gaff the whole thing off. Let Walt and his cronies find another errand boy. It wasn't in him to do that. In for a penny; in for a pound.

"Assuming the KNP buys into this and doesn't shoot my ass on sight, what then?"

"And then you go along with them to the pickup point we designate near the border. We get Chesa and her sister. They get the gold."

The conference call lasted another hour while Walter Ngo and Chris Anthony outlined what details they had in a basic plan. The whole deal involved a lot of back-and-forth. Studying a topo map Anthony spread on the conference table, Shake used his fingers to measure the distances. "The way it looks, Rangoon to Myawaddy, the ville across from Mae Sot on the Thai side, is 400 K give or take. That's a lot of jungle…"

"There's a commercial helicopter outfit that's been laid on to take you to the border where you pick up the sample payment. Gotta be that way. We can't have you trying to clear customs here in Bangkok or in Rangoon with a thirty-pound bar of pure gold in your luggage."

Shake could hear Walt Ngo rattling a keyboard on his end of the call. "We've got a solid guide that will meet you in Myawaddy, Shake. Good man; ex-Army. He's a Karen Burmese that Chesa hired a year ago. Been working with her on the refugee efforts."

"And you trust this guy?"

"Name's Pa Yet. He was wounded when he arrived at the Mae Sot camp. Hit a land mine and was about to lose a leg. Chesa and the docs saved the knee, but they had to amputate one foot and a good part of the lower leg. Chesa got him a prosthetic and helped him rehab. He loves her. He's got an SUV of some kind and he'll take you to Moulmein. That should be familiar to a Kipling fan like you, Shake. *The old Moulmein Pagoda, lookin' lazy at the sea...*"

"And that's where I meet with the KNP honchos?"

"Yes." Chris Anthony tapped a spot on the map. "We'll have an exact location for you shortly. I'd expect they'll send some kind of security detail with you back to the border where they'll verify that we're holding up our end of the bargain. At that point, you take charge of Chesa and get her and her sister safely across the border to Mae Sot."

"Where I'll be waiting." Walt Ngo said. "I'm leaving shortly to make final arrangements for the gold transfer. And I'm bringing cash for you. Greenbacks you can use to ease through any logjams along the way."

"One final question." Shake scratched at the white hair flowing over his ears. He needed to get that mop cut if he was headed for the jungles. "Given the way you've got this thing running and the fact that we're not dealing with bone-in-the-nose headhunters anymore, seems like Mr. Anthony or any other corporate courier could handle the job. Why do you need me?"

Shake heard Walter Ngo breathing deeply over the speaker phone connection. "It's Burma, Shake. Who knows what kind of crap these people might try to pull on one end or the other? I need someone light on his feet, someone who can fight his way through and save Chesa no matter what happens."

When Walter Ngo disconnected, Shake spent another hour or two with Chris Anthony noting what was expected of him over the next few days. He was to fly from Bangkok to Rangoon, clear customs, and check into a hotel. Then he was scheduled for an appointment with something called the Myanmar State Ministry of Religious Affairs and Culture where he would present his Lancer creds and a basic letter outlining what he was supposedly doing for the company on the trip. That was basic legend building.

Next was the chartered helo flight to Myawaddy where he'd either cross into Thailand at Mae Sot or someone from the Thai side would meet him on the Burma side of border with the first installment of the ransom in gold. Then Pa Yet would drive him through 120 miles of jungle to Mawlamyine…or Moulmein if the guy was a Kipling fan.

Anthony was unsure how Shake and the KNP reps would get from Moulmein back to the border for the hostage-gold exchange. Probably some form of heavily armed convoy was his guess. More details to come in the form of regular phone updates.

Anthony handed over a sophisticated satellite phone with attendant chargers and current converters. Shake got a thorough tutorial on its use and assurances that the phone would work even in the most remote locations. If he could see the sky, the phone would find a satellite and put him right through to any of a list of numbers pre-programmed in its memory.

A secretary stepped into the conference room to inform Anthony that a car was standing by to take Shake to the Mandarin Hotel in Bangkok where he was booked for the night.

"You leave for Yangon tomorrow at 5 p.m." Anthony laid a ticket for a Thai International flight on top of the phone support equipment. We'll pick you up at the Mandarin three hours before the flight." He pointed at the package containing the sat phone and accessories. "Charge that tonight and call me later for a test. We'll be talking regularly as things continue to develop."

Shake took one last look at the gleaming gold bar. It was still hard for him to believe that 30-plus pounds of yellow metal could be worth so much. He'd forgotten about the gold standard that once backed world currency—if he ever knew anything about the subject at all.

"Next time you see this beauty…" Anthony patted the gold bar. "…will be in Myawaddy or Mae Sot. We're rigging a false-bottom camera case for you to carry on the trip to meet with the KNP."

Bangkok traffic, especially in the Central Business District, was still the world standard for horrible driving conditions. It took Shake and his driver nearly a full hour to negotiate the two miles from Lancer Tech to the Mandarin Hotel through a noisy, bumper-to-bumper blockade on the city streets.

A lovely little concierge who said she learned her English at UC San Diego and talked like a transplanted surfer girl welcomed him to the Mandarin. Shake couldn't help staring. She looked like a teenage version of his wife, and he was stunned for a long moment before he recovered enough to ask about a haircut. The concierge was smiley and helpful as she handed out brochures and made Shake an appointment for a steam bath and haircut in the hotel spa.

In his room on the Mandarin's 12th floor, he tossed his gear on the bed, plugged in the sat phone charger, and headed down to get himself clear of road dust and mental fog. He fell asleep in the sauna and had to be roused by an attendant who led him into the hair salon. He didn't have much inclination to fuss over styling. "Too much hair. Too hot. Cut it down." Then he ignored what was happening with comb and scissors, closed his eyes, and reviewed what he knew of the mission ahead.

Lots of moving parts at this point, granted. But from the errand boy slash courier slash bodyguard perspective, it seemed relatively simple. If something involving multiple variables, unknowns, volatile players, and lives at risk could ever be called simple. And that's what had Shake worried. In his experience nothing that seemed simple and straightforward ever turned out to be either.

Getting himself set up and running a clandestine legend was nothing new and not as challenging as other times he'd had to operate in similar circumstances. Walt Ngo and Chris Anthony seemed to have the transport and logistics aspects well covered. But there was a whole hell of a lot of jungle between the border and the meet with the KNP at Moulmein, and then back to the border again with hostages in tow. And that area was full of unpredictable and potentially violent bad asses plus who knew how many Burmese Army patrols policing the tribal lands. At encounters like that his video-game designer legend would have to hold and likely cost him plenty of Walt Ngo's cash.

He needed to know more about both the bad-asses and the Army before he'd feel ready to make the trip on his own while carrying 30 pounds of pure gold. Shake made a mental note to call Major Sherman Semple for an appointment as soon as possible after he arrived in Rangoon. What he'd get from a Marine like Semple was likely reliable intelligence he could use.

He decided not to mention meeting with the military liaison to Ngo or Anthony. They'd made it crystal clear that there was a serious risk involving freeloaders, interlopers, or any other kind of official involvement. Apparently the KNP leaders had been very specific about that. Any form of government interference or intervention and the deal was ended—along with the lives of the hostages.

Shorn down to a modified crewcut, Shake ate a solid meal of *tom young goong* over sticky rice in the Mandarin dining room. Sipping chilled fruit juice that would have been tastier with a slug of gin, Shake fired up his laptop, connected to the hotel wi-fi, and dug back into Major Semple's background document on Burmese officialdom. The Army—known as the Tatmadaw—had units in outposts dotted throughout the countryside. They were mainly light infantry and mobile, moving around through the tribal areas in a half-hearted attempt to keep some semblance of peace and quell anti-government resistance. They were also thoroughly corrupt, according to Major Semple. Underpaid, overworked, and not very reliable in garrison or in the field. Surviving an encounter with them was usually just a matter of a credible story and a wad of cash.

Worse than the Tatmadaw were the Border Police and auxiliary guards who were mostly former anti-government rebels that played both ends from the middle. Best bet, Shake decided, is to avoid contact with anyone in Burma but the KNP. Hopefully, Major Sherman would have a tip or two on how to do that.

On his way to the elevators, Shake passed a hotel shop where he spotted a gaudy rack of videogames on display. He browsed for a while, noting most of the action-oriented titles were Lancer Tech products featuring wartime scenarios or superhero adventures. He bought an armful and carried them up to his room. If cash or gold didn't get him out of a jam, maybe a top-flight videogame would serve. Couldn't hurt to have a little insurance in his pocket.

Moulmein

The last part of their trek was in a rattletrap old truck, packed in the back with barrels of fuel oil. Their captors' mood had brightened considerably. Most of them spent the trip laughing and trying to cop feels of the women's breasts and thighs. Chesa slapped the grimy hands away angrily. Endra just wiggled and giggled. Chesa vowed to make some serious corrections in her sister's behavior as soon as they reached Moulmein.

The truck finally ground to a halt on the outskirts of the town. It was nearly dark, but as she was pulled off the tailgate, Chesa saw the towering, ornate pagoda that was the showpiece of Moulmein. So, they were in Mon State. She'd visited once with her parents to pray at the *stupa* which she later learned had been made semi-famous by a Rudyard Kipling poem.

A well-dressed man in western clothing emerged from the shadows and spoke to Pak. Chesa and her sister were muscled forward to confront the man who simply looked them over carefully when Pak handed over her passport and cell phone.

"You are Chesa," he said in English. "Mrs. Chesa Ngo, wife of Walter Ngo, the President and CEO of Lancer Technologies?"

Chesa could see what was coming now. She was a hostage held for ransom. There didn't seem to be any point in denying it. "I am Chesa Ngo, an American citizen. This is my sister Endra."

The man rubbed his bald head and smiled. "Just so," he said. "We are in contact with your husband."

"Who is we?" Chesa interrupted angrily.

"The Karen National Progressive Party of Myanmar, Mrs. Ngo. You will be our guests until arrangements have been completed with your husband."

"What arrangements?"

"A simple trade. You and your sister in exchange for some things we need very badly to continue our struggle."

"And Walter…my husband…has agreed to this?" Chesa had never let her husband know she knew about it, but he was having serious financial and business problems. Walter would have to do some painful things to meet a big ransom demand. She was suddenly feeling very guilty about all the money she'd asked him to spend on their refugee efforts.

"Oh, yes. Mister Ngo is very anxious to have you back safe and sound. It will be a matter of days now. We have established certain deadlines. My name is Pha Pat, I am chairman of the Party here in Moulmein. If you will follow me, we have bathing facilities and fresh clothing for you and your sister."

They were led into a two-story cinderblock building that appeared to sit in an isolated space outside the dusty sprawl of Moulmein. There were armed guards strolling the grounds, but one-eyed Pak and his men had disappeared into the night.

When they entered a large anteroom, two female guards appeared. They were beefy women with dark eyes and grim expressions. Short, sharp knives hung at their waists. "These women will escort you to the bathing area," Pha Pat said with a wave in their direction. Then his voice changed to a growl. "We will try to make you and your sister comfortable, Mrs. Ngo, but let me make one thing clear. You are prisoners of the KNP. We will tolerate no resistance or bad behavior while we wait for your husband to comply with our demands."

"And if he doesn't?" Chesa couldn't resist asking even though she knew the answer to her question. They might be prisoners for a long time before Walter managed to raise the ransom demand. He would have to scramble, maybe even sell off his controlling interest in the company he'd built.

"You should understand something, Mrs. Ngo. The KNP fights to be free of the butchers and criminals in Yangon. To unify the resistance to their illegitimate junta. To be the masters of our own fate rather than slaves to an illegitimate government. Your abduction is a part of that fight. If your husband gives us the means to continue our struggle, you are free, and we fight on with renewed capabilities. If he fails to meet our demands, you and your sister will disappear into the jungle, never to be seen or heard from again."

Rangoon

It was just after 10 p.m. by the time Shake shoved and sweated his way through the throng at Yangon International Airport immigration and customs. Everything in and outside the terminal building seemed to be lit with an eye-watering blaze of purple or pink neon. A clearly bored immigration official at the desk grunted a question while holding his rubber stamp poised over Shake's passport. Here for business? Yes, indeed, thank you, sir. And the stamp fell followed by a wave that told Shake to get moving.

During the sat phone check call with Chris Anthony, he'd been instructed to take a shuttle for the 35-kilometer ride from the airport to the Lotte Hotel in the city center. Shake was shoe-horned into a little mini-bus with only a few other passengers. All looked like well-heeled Asian businessmen carrying expensive travel bags and aluminum laptop cases. Apparently, the Lotte Hotel was not for bargain-hunters or student backpackers.

He was mobbed at the hotel entrance by a crowd of uniformed minions that scrapped over the honor of carrying Shake's old jungle rucksack inside. The losers settled for handing him bar or restaurant brochures before they assaulted the next passenger to dismount from the shuttle.

Shake felt slightly out of place in cargo trousers, boots, and a tattered old safari jacket, but the slick little man at the reception desk didn't seem to notice once he got a swipe from the Amex Platinum credit card Chris Anthony had included with Shake's travel documents. He'd been assured it would work anywhere. The name Shake Davis had been added to the authorized user list. The desk man handed over a keycard and a scented embossed envelope bearing Shake's name and room number. The note was from one Pha Aung, Cultural Affairs Minister at the Myanmar State Ministry of Religious Affairs and Culture, who would be honored to meet with Mr. Davis of Lancer Technologies at 10 a.m. There was an address listed which the reception desk man said was just a moderate walk or a short taxi ride from the hotel.

Shake stopped by the concierge desk on his way to the elevators and got a number for the American Embassy. He'd be delighted to meet with Pha Aung, but what he really wanted to do before heading into the hinterlands was spend a little time with Major Sherman Semple. He called the number and tapped his way through the Embassy phone tree. When he reached Semple's extension, the voice asking him to leave a message had a raw, over-stressed edge. This guy had probably done some time as a DI or tactics instructor at some point in his career. Shake left a message plus call back number.

He spent an hour or so between a long shower and repacking his gear with the videogames and tech support equipment he'd picked up along the way to Rangoon. Then he sprawled in skivvies and fell asleep listening to a cranky air conditioner wheeze, wondering just how much about what he was really doing in Burma he could afford to reveal, even to a kindred spirit like Major Semple.

His new phone buzzed while Shake was muddling toast through runny egg yolk at a table in the hotel restaurant. Major Sherman Semple's growl had a pleasant edge to it.

"Shake Davis…retired Marine Gunner." It was not a question. "Thought I recognized the name. I dragged an old buddy of mine out of the rack back stateside to check on you. Seems you've got a pretty serious rep in our little gun club."

"Well, you know how that goes, Major. War stories tend to get exaggerated."

"Couldn't make up some of the shit I heard about you, Gunner. What are you doing in the Republic of the Union of Myanmar?"

"Working for a tech outfit…kind of. I'll tell you more if you've got a few minutes to meet today."

"I'm clearing the decks right now. We don't get many distinguished Marines visiting this cesspool, so let's have a few beers and tell war stories."

"I've got an appointment later this morning. How about we meet somewhere for lunch?"

Semple rattled off the name and location of a place between the Rangoon River and Inya Lake that was relatively close to them both and gave Shake his personal cell number. Shake paid his bill and headed for a little ready-made clothing outlet he'd spotted near the hotel. He'd need to wear something less paramilitary and more business casual for the meeting with the Burmese ministry official. He shopped mindlessly for an hour, plucking khaki trousers, a white shirt, and a lightweight blue blazer from the racks. His mind was on the game of duck and dodge he'd have to play later with Major Sherman Semple.

Back at the hotel, he pulled the tags from his new clothes, changed, and shaved. As an afterthought as he was leaving for his appointment, he tucked three or four of the videogames bought in Bangkok into a pocket. A good salesman doesn't hit the road without samples.

His phone twittered when he was about a block away from the ministry headquarters. He ducked under a streetside café umbrella for some shade and heard Chris Anthony on the line.

"You OK?"

"All good so far, just heading for the meet with the cultural guy. How is it on your end?"

"Walt got in late last night. We're heading up-country later today to make some arrangements. Looks like you'll have to come across from Myawaddy to Mae Sot for the pick-up. Shouldn't be a problem. We'll have the skids greased by the time you get there."

"OK…just let me know how it works when you know. Anything else from Moulmein?"

"Yeah. Our friends are getting antsy. Wanting to know when we'll come through. Some threats this time. They think we're stalling."

"Well, shit, Chris. I'm just following instructions."

"We know that. They don't. But we assured them our rep was in country and headed their way. Gave them an ETA of 72 hours from now, so don't get bulldozed over there. If there's any kind of unavoidable delay, let me know right away."

"Planning on leaving ASAP. Just need to get this meeting done. You guys got the helo to Myawaddy laid on?"

"All set. It's an outfit called HeliUnion, on the commercial side of YIA. Tomorrow morning at seven they'll fly you Rangoon to Myawaddy. Cross over to Mae Sot, where you'll meet with the guide and then back over to the Burma side. We've got it all dialed in for you."

"Walt's wife and sister still OK?"

"Far as we know. He wanted to speak to her on the last call, but they weren't having it. He's getting worried."

As Shake climbed the marble steps leading into the State Ministry of Religious Affairs and Culture, he was wondering about rip-offs, reversals, and scams. What if he got to Moulmein carrying the gold and found the hostages dead? He didn't like the odds of getting out of it alive. What he wanted, what would make him feel a bit better about the odds, was a weapon. Nothing big or imposing. Just something reliable he could use to leverage himself out of a tight spot. He was most comfortable with some version of old slab-sides, a 1911 or clone in .45 ACP. He'd ask Semple about that if he could work it into their conversation.

Mr. Pha Aung's office was the only one at the end of a long corridor that reeked of sandalwood incense. He couldn't decipher the Burmese script on the door. It looked like a series of pictographs produced by some weird kid's Etch A Sketch. But Minister Pha Aung's name and title in English were there in gold leaf print, so Shake pushed open the door and stepped into an anteroom which appeared to be the domain of a nut-brown woman in a gilded vest over a long tubular skirt.

"Help you, please?" The woman rose, folded her hands under her chin and bowed. Her English was heavily accented and seemed to be sung rather than spoken. She was likely a stunning beauty, but her face and arms had Shake momentarily speechless. Her cheeks and forehead were painted with some sort of off-white powder or cream. If he squinted—which he couldn't help doing at the moment—it looked like someone had painted little leaves with prominent veins in a triangle pattern on her face.

"You are Mr. Davis?" She repeated the little prayer bow before Shake could do much more than nod. "Please to take a seat." She waved a hand painted with the same patterns toward a cluster of chairs in the opposite corner of the anteroom. "Minister Aung just finishing a call. He will be available very soon."

Shake slumped into a chair and tried to focus on the letter of introduction he was to deliver, but he couldn't help looking over at the Burmese receptionist or secretary. She just smiled showing a row of perfect white teeth and looked him over carefully.

"It's my first visit to Bur…uh, Myanmar. Could I ask about…" He waved a hand vaguely in her direction, but she seemed to know what he was asking.

"We call it *thanaka*. Traditional make-up for Bamar people." She smiled and turned her head so Shake could get the full effect. It was exotic and as becoming as it was strange. "Today *thanaka* is mostly worn by women and young girls." She covered her mouth with a painted hand and giggled. "Saves very much on lipstick."

"Very pretty." Shake was searching for something to add when the inner office door opened, and he was confronted by a stumpy little man in tinted eyeglasses, wearing a flowing saffron-colored robe. Shake had seen enough Buddhist monks in his Southeast Asia time to know one when he saw one.

The man's plastic sandals slapped on the tile floor as he advanced with a hand extended. "So sorry for the delay," he said in a clipped accent with Oxford overtones. "I am Pha Aung. Please come into my office."

Aung motioned toward a chair facing his desk. "Can I offer you tea? Or perhaps you'd prefer a soft drink?"

"No, thank you." Shake was still a little shaken by what he was seeing of the minister and his minion. "I've just eaten…and my business is pressing." Maybe culture shock, he decided, and tried to keep from staring. Nothing he'd seen so far in Rangoon so far matched this pair.

Aung seemed to sense what was on his visitor's mind. "As a minister of religious and cultural affairs," he said with a beaming smile. "I like to present visitors with a look at our Bamar culture."

"So, you're a monk as well as a government minister?"

"The two are not mutually exclusive, Mr. Davis. Yangon is a devoutly Buddhist country. I serve the way of the Buddha and the way of my government with no conflict." He accepted the letter Shake handed him and read for a moment.

"You are a designer of videogames. In Myanmar doing research for a new project?"

"Yes, sir." Shake nodded and smiled, hoping to look like a tech-nerd, as Aung adjusted his glasses and turned back to the letter. "I see…I see. A game that will feature my country when it was Burma, a major battleground during the Second World War."

"That's right. I need to photograph some of the country so our designers can recreate it accurately in the game."

"And when someone plays this game, he will be one of General Wingate's Chindits? Or perhaps an American with General Merrill's…what is it? Maulers?"

"Marauders. Very famous unit. Made it very tough on the Japanese occupation forces in this country." Apparently, Minister Pha Aung's education included a pretty stiff dose of military history. "I'm impressed that you know about the Chindits and Merrill's Marauders. They often don't get as much mention as other units that fought in Europe or in the Pacific island campaigns."

"Yes…unfortunate. The fighting in my country was very intense—and very important to the allied victory."

"Very true, Minister. It's one of the reasons we are so anxious to make this new videogame."

Aung pondered with pursed lips. "And do you think there might be room in this game for a Bamar fighter? Maybe a local hero who helps the British and Americans?" Pha Aung grinned and made a pistol out of one chubby hand. He made little *pyew, pyew* sounds as his thumb went up and down and his index finger swept the room.

"I'll be sure to check on that, sir. It's still very early in the research and development process."

"I am familiar with this part of my country's history, you know. There were many Burmese who helped the allies defeat the Japanese."

"I'll recommend it highly, sir. I can promise you that."

With a nod, Aung picked up the letter of introduction. "You plan to go into our jungles to photograph, is that correct?"

"Well, yes…focusing on areas where the fighting actually took place. Our artists will want to create the country as it looks...or looked back then."

"Very good…very nice." Aung plucked a piece of paper from a folder on his desk and handed it over to Shake. Apparently, a decision about clearance for his trip had already been made. "We support such efforts fully. We want people to understand that Myanmar is a good place filled with good people. There has been too much negative and false information about us in the world press lately."

Shake glanced at the letter in his hand. He recognized mention of Lancer Technologies and the United States but nothing else. The body of the text was in those quaint Burmese characters. "Thank you for this, Minister."

"The letter gives a guarantee of government support and approval for your project. Should someone question it, they need only call the number listed at the bottom. I will promptly clear up any confusion."

"Hopefully, there won't be any, Minister. I will be with an experienced guide at all times."

"Good. But I should warn you. In some areas we are experiencing anti-government activities. It would be best for you to avoid those areas." The Minister stood and extended a hand. Shake shook it and stood to leave.

"I have a nephew," Minster Pha Aung said as they walked toward the door. "He plays videogames every waking moment. A very bright child."

"Perhaps your nephew would enjoy this." Shake reached into his blazer and pulled out a copy of *Spearhead,* a new Lancer release that advertised a wild ride with Patton's 3rd Army in the drive to the Rhine.

"He most assuredly will!" Aung took the plastic-cased game like he was handed a precious gem and chuckled. "And I will become his favorite uncle!"

On the way out, the painted receptionist tinkled a little laugh and handed Shake a pocket-size booklet outlining various aspects of Myanmar and Burmese culture. She'd paper-clipped a section of it that dealt with *thanaka.* Shake winked at her and dropped a copy of a game called *She-ra, Goddess of the Jungle* on her desk.

ၰၰ

He was early for his luncheon meeting with Major Sherman Semple, so Shake consulted a street map and started walking toward Inya Lake, confident he could find the Floating Lotus restaurant once he got there. Minister Pha Aung indicated Burma was a devoutly Buddhist country and everything he saw seemed to confirm that. Every man or woman he passed on the street seemed to be wearing a necklace of fine gold suspending a Buddha image or religious symbol related to

Buddhism. Little statues or shrines were tucked into any spare space and fronted by ceramic jars that sprouted incense sticks. And on a nearby hilltop, towering over the city architecture, was the Shwedagon Pagoda. There was a description of it in the booklet Aung's receptionist gave him and Shake paused at a street corner to read. The huge golden dome was also called the Great Dragon or Golden Pagoda and dated from some time in the 14th Century. It was apparently a classic and very famous *stupa,* said to contain physical relics of the earliest Buddha Gautama and some of his successors. Probably a great place to visit and explore if he had the time. But he didn't.

The Floating Lotus Restaurant was easy to spot once he reached the lake shore. It was a sprawling joint that shared space with a row of shop fronts and occupied most of the little spear of land between the lake and the banks of the Yangon River. There was a long stretch of outdoor café tables under colorful sun umbrellas close to the riverbank, many of them occupied by tourists and backpackers. Shake selected a remote table with a good view of the muddy river waters, ordered a cold Singha beer and checked his watch. He still had a half hour before his embassy contact was due to arrive, so he hauled out the tourist brochure and began to read.

There was a lot of nationalist hucksterism letting visitors know that Myanmar was just short of a paradise on earth but what caught his attention was the stuff about the Burmese jungles. And it seemed like most of Burma outside the bigger towns and cities was jungle. Most of that was the tropical rainforest variety. Someone had apparently counted the flora and fauna. The brochure claimed Myanmar was home to 16,000 plant varieties. And if you wanted to see wildlife, there were 314 mammals of one type or another including rhinoceros, water buffalo, leopards, wild boar, antelope, and elephants. Nice to see a rhino or an elephant in the wild, but he could do without running into the crocodiles, cobras, or Burmese pythons who also thrived in the local jungles.

Major Sherman Semple came dodging through the tables like a running back searching for an open field. He waved when he spotted Shake. Neither Shake nor Semple seemed to have any doubts about who was who even if the Marine officer was wearing a lightweight civilian suit. Takes one to know one. Shake stood up and extended a hand.

"Had you pegged all the way," Semple grinned and flopped into a chair opposite Shake. He glanced at Shake's beer and checked a Rolex Submariner on his wrist. "Sun's over the yardarm somewhere, I guess." He waved to a waiter.

"Might be the haircut," Shake said. "Had it cut down in Bangkok, but the barber was clueless about high and tight."

Semple laughed and pulled a photo out of his jacket pocket. He slid it across the table and Shake saw it was a copy of one of his old official portraits taken when he was on active duty. The stack of ribbons over his left pocket seemed gaudy even to the man who earned them. "Pal of mine pulled it from the files, Gunner. Like I said, you're well known in certain circles. Don't mind me saying so, it's an honor to meet you."

They established a first-name basis which forced him to explain how Sheldon became Shake when he was rapidly advanced in the enlisted ranks causing his peers to consider him a Shake 'n Bake NCO. It was Shake and Sherm as they spent the next half-hour and two more beers over war stories, trying to establish links to people they knew in the Corps. Standard drill among Marines. It was mostly Semple asking about tales he'd heard concerning Shake's service in

Vietnam, Beirut, and Central America. Too many of the men Semple mentioned as knowing or serving with Shake turned out to be dead.

"I'm after some information that I can use on a trip I'm taking up-country," Shake said when a third round appeared on the table. "I read a report you wrote. Very interesting."

"I write a lot of reports, Shake. Damn near all I do these days."

"I think you'd remember this one. Written last year. Had some pretty hard words to say about Burma officialdom, the Army…"

Semple leaned across the table and lowered his voice to a whisper. "You read that? Damn near got me fired. The Ambassador was some kind of pissed. I thought they stamped it classified and buried it."

"Well, some friends of mine unearthed it, I guess. Anyway, it goes no further than me. I just want some tips from a guy who sees the truth and isn't afraid to tell it."

Semple sat back and toyed with his beer bottle. He eyed the man sitting across from him carefully. "How about we make a deal here. I'll tell you anything I can—straight scoop, Marine to Marine—if you do the same with me."

"OK by me." Shake shrugged and hit his beer.

Semple leaned back across the table. "You CIA?"

"Negative. And not State or any other government agency either."

"Who you working for over here?"

"Sherm, I'm under an NDA. The outfit paying the bills is Lancer Technologies out of Las Vegas. They produce videogames and I'm supposed to be collecting local scenery for a game they want to produce. I can't tell you much more than that, but rest assured it's a private enterprise, no government, or military connections whatever."

"You said that's what you're *supposed* to be doing. And that tells me you're really doing something else, right?"

"That's where the NDA comes into play, Sherm."

"That's pretty thin, Shake."

"I know it is. Like I said, officially I'm gathering information and local color for a game about Chindits and Merrill's Marauders in Burma during World War II. There's more to it—and that's the part I can't tell you about."

Semple sat back and tapped a finger on the glass tabletop. "Well, I gotta believe a man like you wouldn't sell out to the dark side. Law enforcement? Drug trafficking in this slice of the Golden Triangle?"

"Not my concern, Sherm."

"You know this shithole is second only to Afghanistan in producing raw opium. And Burma has more meth labs out there in the jungle than anyone can count."

"That's what I got from your report, Sherm. But it's not what I'm after. Let's just say I'm trying to save a life and hoping that doing that will be the extent of my stay in Burma."

"You know if you get caught doing something illegal over here, even something that just pisses off the Burmese government for one reason or another, I can't help you."

"Just some straight information about the game and the players out in the jungles, Sherm. That's all I'm asking…beyond your trust that I'll stay low-profile and I'm not doing anything illegal."

Semple polished off his beer and waved for another round. "Well, if you can't trust another Marine, who the fuck can you trust? What do you want to know?"

"Tell me about the Karen National Progressive Party."

They talked for about three more hours, which included a delicious dinner of steamed and spicy seafood. Shake spent most of that time just listening and trying to dodge Semple's subtle probes for more information about his real mission in Burma. The information was scattershot but free flowing. Semple talked like he wrote about the subjects with no punches pulled. When the question of obtaining a weapon arose, Semple laughed and waved his hand expansively. "Shit, Shake. You're in the Walmart of weapons out in those jungles. Find the right guy, flash some cash, and you wind up with practically anything that goes bang."

"Yeah…but how do I find the right guy?"

"It ain't hard. You see a dude wandering around out there and packing something you want, just ask him to sell it to you for cash. He can get another weapon a whole lot easier than he can get cash money."

Semple finished his beer and checked his watch again. It was just before local sunset. "Which begs the question…if you're not doing anything shady, how come you want a weapon?"

Shake picked up the tourist brochure and waved it. "Says right here I might encounter crocs, cobras, or the dreaded Burmese python."

"Better buy yourself enough gun!"

"No mouse guns for me, Sherm. If it ain't got a four and a five in the nomenclature, I don't want it."

As night descended on Rangoon, Shake was walking back to his hotel hoping he was sober enough to tap out a synopsis of what he'd learned on his laptop. It was valuable information and needed study, especially the insights on the Karen National Progressive Party. They were upstart nationalists, founded in 2021, a clever amalgam of brute muscle and canny politicians, all vehemently anti-Rangoon government. What made them a little different than the average anti-Rangoon faction was the relative sophistication in their leadership coupled with cutthroat capabilities in their muscle factions. Unlike many other nationalist or tribal organizations in the Burmese countryside, the KNP was backed by some relatively sophisticated, well-educated people, and fronted by a very ruthless band of jungle-savvy guerillas. A powerful combination that kept the KNP near the top of a crush of competing tribal groups in the Burmese hinterlands.

As he turned a corner at the street leading to his hotel, he was blanketed with a cloud of rich incense. An older woman was standing at one of the little Buddhist shrines, head bowed, and hands clasped around a burning incense stick. She was likely pushing sixty with glossy black hair cascading over her shoulders and nearly reaching her waist. She wore an embroidered tube skirt and a beaded blouse, an outfit that toed a line between conservative and sensual. When she turned away from her prayers, the woman glanced at him. The skin at the corners of her dark eyes crinkled as she smiled. Probably just how Chan would have looked if she'd lived.

Shake put some *kyat* coins into the bowl at the base of the little altar, selected a joss stick, and lit it. As the fragrant smoke ascended into the night air, he hoped somehow Chan would know he was thinking of her.

After a half hour at his laptop back in the hotel room, Shake saved what he'd written, opened a new document, and tapped out a complete description of what he was doing in Burma—all details, full disclosure. When the time was right, after he'd done the deal and rescued Chesa Ngo and her sister, he'd send it along to Major Sherman Semple.

Myawaddy

As he was waiting in a lounge on the commercial side of Yangon International, Shake's sat phone buzzed. Walt Ngo calling from somewhere in Thailand. Shake punched up the connection and moved to a remote corner away from the dispatch clerk at the HeliUnion desk.

"Where are you?"

"Right where I'm supposed to be, Walt. Waiting for a helicopter. Should be up at Myawaddy in a couple hours."

"Best we can do, I guess…"

"What's the problem?

"Heard from the assholes at Moulmein. They're getting nervous about delays. Seem to think we're setting up to pull some kind of stunt. Lots of threats…said they'll up the asking price if we don't get a move on."

"They're not likely to do something stupid…"

"Hopefully, they won't. They've given up on the weapons list, thank God. And that's a big step forward for us. But a mil in gold is hard to move below the radar."

"Well, if they buy into your scheme, they'll wind up with more than they're asking anyway, right?"

"Yeah. Market price is up right now, but you've got to convince them of that. Tell them what's waiting for them at the border will be worth what they're asking now."

"Damn, Walt—I'm no financial expert. You want me to sit up there and argue market prices with these guys?"

"I'm putting together some documents for you. Some real-world values and exchange rates. It's solid stuff that they'll recognize as the real deal. The way we've got it figured, the final delivery will price out at around one-point-four by the time they lay hands on it."

"What happens if they don't buy into the deal?"

"I don't know, Shake. Honestly, I really don't know. But they seemed anxious to get Chesa and her sister off their hands. They let me talk to her for a couple of seconds this time."

"She OK?"

"Just sounded scared and exhausted. She knows we're in a tough spot, but she's holding out."

Shake caught a signal from the dispatch desk and heard the whine of jet engines spooling up on the ramp outside the building. "Gotta go, Walt. The helo's ready. Guess we'll talk again when I get up to the border."

"Right. Soon as you can, call me and come across Number 2 Friendship Bridge. You shouldn't have any trouble if you just flash your passport and tell them you're going shopping in Mae Sot. I'll meet you at the Irrawaddy Resort. It's not far from the border crossing. Anyone can tell you how to get here."

"Copy all. See you in a little while."

As Shake pocketed the phone and shouldered his rucksack, a short, stocky man wearing aviator shades and a tailored flight suit approached. "You'd likely be my passenger for Myawaddy." He extended a calloused hand. "Name's Ian Cuthbert. Just call me Chunky."

Shake shook hands and gave his name as they walked outside to the waiting helicopter with blades just beginning to turn. "Nice bird, Chunky. Sikorsky?"

The pilot pulled open the passenger door and Shake caught sight of a copilot in the right seat. They had to shout over the turbine whine and clatter as the blades whirled up to speed. "An S-76—got the range we need. Good airspeed and stability." As Shake climbed aboard, Chunky Cuthbert pointed at a headset hanging from a clip on the overhead and patted his ears. "Talk more when we get airborne."

The helicopter was clearly set up as some kind of executive taxi. It featured upholstered seats and little built-in folding tables next to a rack of water bottles and soda cans. Damn sight different than the rattletrap Hueys and Phrogs he was used to riding inbound to missions in the jungle. Shake settled in as the aircraft began to taxi toward the active runway and donned the headset. He heard Chunky identify the flight to the tower and ask for clearance to lift and a northbound departure. After a few minutes idling on an access ramp, the pilots pulled pitch and the helicopter broke contact with the ground. Shake felt the familiar gravity press in his hips and stomach as the Sikorsky dipped and then clawed up into the muggy air over Rangoon.

"Seen a few whirlybirds in your time, have you?" Chunky's voice over the headset had a clipped British lilt. Shake mentally pegged him as ex-RAF. "Saw your pack and bet Jolly you were ex-military." The man in the right seat turned to look back and smiled giving Shake a thumbs-up. "Name's Jolly Withers," he said over the intercom. "Welcome aboard."

"Thanks." Shake reached for a sweaty bottle of water and unscrewed the cap. "Got some time in helos but none as nice as this one."

Jolly got a tower hand off to departure control for a cruising altitude and heading for Myawaddy. As his copilot fiddled with the radios, Chunky turned and cupped his hand around a Zippo to light a cigarette.

"Smoke 'em if you got 'em. We don't hold much with FAA regs over here."

Shake reached into his vest pocket and held up a can of Copenhagen. He'd started to bring some cigars, but his old bush instinct told him to rely on a dip or two if he needed a nicotine fix.

"Nasty stuff." Chunky exhaled a plume of smoke and shook his head. "But you GIs eat it like candy."

"Old habits die hard, I guess."

"You U.S. Army?" Jolly's voice also had British overtones but Shake heard some differences. He decided the co-pilot was likely South African.

"U.S. Marine Corps." Shake rolled a pinch into his lower lip and savored the familiar burn.

"Extra careful, Jolly…" Chunky punched his copilot on the shoulder. "We've got a bloody bootneck aboard."

"I'm guessing you guys must be ex-RAF, right?"

"Half right." Chunky turned to glance at the instrument panel to confirm they were at their assigned altitude and on the proper northerly heading. "I flew choppers in Her Majesty's forces for about ten years. Jolly here got his tickets in South Africa flying commando forces on anti-terrorist ops out of Jo-burg. Barely competent…"

"Fuck off, Chunky." Jolly lifted a hand from the collective and extended two fingers, in the British version of a middle digit. "You'll give the man the wrong impression."

Both pilots returned to their business and rolled the helicopter onto a new heading that came in from a controller somewhere on the ground.

"That course correction puts us on a direct line to Myawaddy, mate." Chunky pointed at the windscreen. "Should be on the ground up there in a little less than two hours."

"And then you head back to Rangoon?"

"That's the agenda. We'll put down at a little airstrip just west of Myawaddy town, refuel and R-T-B. You staying long up at the border?"

"Not too long, I hope. Supposed to get some photos of the countryside for my bosses…that kind of thing."

"Be careful doing that, mate. Great bunch of bandits out there in the jungle. Shoot you for your camera in a trice, no questions asked or answered."

"I'll do my best to avoid that kind of thing." Shake settled back and watched the ground rushing past below the helicopter. It was a sea of verdant green. Nothing but jungle interspersed with little settlements. Occasionally he caught sight of a farmer trundling through a little open patch behind a yoked water buffalo. It seemed very familiar, a lot like the view from a helo flying over the Vietnamese countryside. When he was flying those routes, he was painfully aware that there was always someone down in that lush terrain waiting to kill him. From what he'd heard about the turmoil in the Burmese countryside, it was probably not much different. He shook that thought off and started wondering how Walt Ngo and Chris Anthony planned to get him back across the bridge from Mae Sot, Thailand to Myawaddy in Burma with enough pure gold to get him jailed or killed outright in a fight over possession of such rare riches.

Two hours later Chunky and Jolly expertly put the Sikorsky down on a patch of tarmac near a short runway that looked like it might accommodate little commuter aircraft but not much more. As his copilot wandered off to find a refueler, Chunky Cuthbert helped Shake unload his ruck. "Pleasure meeting you, mate." He tapped his chest. "Got a little soft spot in here for you American Marines. Couple of your blokes pulled me out of a tight spot over in the sandbox one bad night. Wouldn't have made it out if they hadn't been on top of the mark and able to keep the baddies at bay."

"Glad they did that for you, Chunky. Otherwise Heli-Union would have lost a damn good pilot."

"You know Jolly and me…we're just marking time over here. We've been known to undertake other jobs, and we own our own little bird for that purpose." Chunky pointed at the camera hanging around Shake's neck. "We fly aerial photo missions, you know. Might suit you one of these days." He handed over a card. "Private number's on the back. Keep us in mind."

Shake pocketed the card, shook hands, and retrieved his rucksack. He headed for a dusty main street and a little space out of the sun where he could check in with his support team across the river in Thailand. Walter Ngo answered on the first ring and told him to proceed across the river into Thailand. They were waiting for him with the ransom down payment packaged and ready to go.

The map indicated Myawaddy was five klicks from his current position. There was only one road visible, so Shake hitched at his ruck and started walking.

Moulmein

T en seconds on the phone is ridiculous!" Chesa hitched at the baggy dress the rebels had provided for her and Endra. It was wonderful to hear Walter's voice and his reassurances that help was on the way, but there was so much more she wanted to say. She wanted to apologize for disobeying, getting them into this fix, but she hadn't said much more than hello and I'm all right before Pha Pat had snatched the phone back from her.

She stood fuming in a corner of the anteroom as Pha Pat continued to talk to her husband. She'd managed to glance at the caller ID on the phone and saw an international number indicating Walter was in Thailand. That was somewhat reassuring, but what she heard next was not.

The conversation between her husband and the rebel leader gave her chills. Speaking in sharp sentences, Pha Pat indicated time was critical. He was tired of delays and suspicious of trickery. He listened for a few moments and then jabbed a finger in the air as if he was talking to someone in person rather than someone on the other side of a phone call.

"Fine," he said. "And if your man does not appear very soon, we no longer have a deal, Mr. Ngo. And you will no longer have a wife."

Chesa sat for a moment watching Pha Pat assemble a few more KNP men for instructions. She couldn't hear his whispered conversation, but he was clearly angry. Was there a problem? Did Walter say something the rebel leader didn't want to hear? She began to piece together what she knew of their current situation. The KNP was asking for money, a lot of it. Walter was in Thailand. Did that mean he'd come to pay what was being asked? And what about the reference to "your man?" Did that indicate Walter was sending someone to negotiate? Would that someone take them back to Thailand?

Earlier in the day, one-eyed Pak had shown back up at the rebel headquarters with his band of guerillas. Pha Pat ordered them to stay nearby. And he mentioned something about two days. She assumed that was how long she and Endra had to live if Walter didn't pay the ransom demand in that time.

When she got back to the dank little room where they slept, Endra was sitting on a pallet, in deep conversation with a bespectacled man she'd never seen before. He was a native Karen. Chesa could tell from his traditional tribal clothing. The man nodded at her and then shook hands formally with Endra.

He nodded wordlessly to Chesa and then padded out the door on bare feet. Chesa sat beside her sister. "I spoke for a little while with my husband. I think he is going to pay what they want to get us released. He is sending someone here to pick us up and take us back to Thailand."

Endra shrugged. Her sister didn't seem very concerned, even though Chesa had made it clear about the jeopardy they faced. "Your husband will pay the money for us?"

"Yes. I think so. He's sending someone right now."

"Well, that's good, isn't it?"

"Yes, Endra, it is. I think we will be free soon." Chesa walked to a window and stood staring at the spire of the Moulmein *stupa* in the distance. Walter was in Thailand but did he manage to raise the necessary funds? And if so, what did he have to sacrifice for them?

Endra sprawled like a house cat on her thin mattress. "And the Karen people will have a lot of money to fight the oppressors in Yangon."

"What? Where did you hear that?"

Endra waved at the door to their room. "I have been talking to Miyat Win. A very learned man, Chesa. He is a leader in the fight to free our people."

Chesa was stunned. It was as if her sister didn't understand what they were facing. "That fight is not our problem right now, Endra. We must survive until we are rescued."

"And then what, sister?" Endra reached for a bottle of water and drank. "What happens to us…to me?"

"You will go with me to Thailand and then to America."

Endra didn't seem very satisfied with that answer, but she nodded and walked over to stare out their small window at the expanse of verdant jungle surrounding their prison.

Myawaddy

Shake smelled the town long before he saw it. Through a stand of wind-warped palm trees, sunlight glinted on a sludgy river that reeked like an open sewer. GPS said it was the Thaung Yi if you were on the Burma side. Moei if you were over in Thailand.

If you've heard the East a-calling, you won't need anything else. Just the spicy garlic smells, and the sunshine and the palm trees and the tinkly temple bells.

For all its dusty, small-town atmosphere, Myawaddy was chock full of gingerbread facades. Shake thought it looked like one of Disneyland's little worlds within the larger park. There were gilded *stupas* with pointy crests along the main drag. And several of the buildings he passed on his way to the Number 2 Friendship Bridge where Chris Anthony told him to cross the river into Thailand had intricate upswept sidings that made them look like Buddhist temples. Lots of carved dragons wrapped around support beams. Lots of smiling Buddhas sitting cross-legged with an open hand raised in benediction. And there were a few gambling dens. Shake heard the rattle and ring of pachinko machines as he passed.

Traffic along the broad main street was what he'd come to think of as typical but relatively sparse at mid-afternoon. There were lots of small Japanese minivans and trucks. Two-stroke bikes and scooters added clouds of exhaust smoke to the muggy air. And all of them seemed to be headed east toward Thailand.

Long lines of tables and stalls lined the road as he neared the bridge. There were a few obvious tourists aiming cameras, but most of the shoppers appeared to be local Burmese after stuff they couldn't get on their side of the river. Merchants accosted pedestrians hawking trade goods fresh from suppliers on the other side of the river. Most of the stuff for sale was Japanese or Chinese origin. Some electronics, lots of knock-off sneakers and t-shirts bearing mistranslated slogans like *Do Fun Plenty*. One of the brochures said gems and precious stones like Burmese rubies moved in the opposite direction for sale to Thai jewelers. Maybe so, but it looked like import vastly outweighed export in Myawaddy commerce.

Chan had always wanted a real Burmese ruby. She raved about the stone's dark, lustrous color. There are rubies and then there are *Burmese* rubies she told him once on a shopping trip when she'd spotted one of the stones in a jeweler's display. *Should have bought the damn thing right then and there, but I didn't*. Shake shook off the pain and brought his focus back to getting across Friendship Bridge No. 2.

Under the arch of the bridge there was what looked like a hobo camp full of women squatting over wood fires and naked kids splashing along the riverbank. It resembled one of LA's ramshackle homeless camps minus the drunks and junkies. A few border cops in mismatched uniform remnants patrolled the area, but they didn't seem overly concerned with the squatters. Probably refugees from the interior looking for a chance to cross into Thailand. Walt Ngo said there were something like nine teeming refugee camps dotted along the border with a population that ran to over 80,000. It was supposedly monitored by something called the Thai-Burma Border Consortium, and Chesa Ngo had worked for that organization.

He was the only white man in a gabbling line of pedestrians heading for the border police checkpoint. Shake noticed most of the Burmese in line were palming *kyat* bills which indicated the free access advertised wasn't free. He pulled a twenty in green and slipped it into his passport. The stack of twenties he had folded in a money clip was getting slim. So far, he'd had to use either his own cash or the Lancer Tech credit card. Hopefully, the expenses he'd covered out of pocket would be replenished as promised when he met with Ngo and Anthony.

The guard who took his passport at the checkpoint palmed the double sawbuck like a lounge show magician, but he didn't execute the pass-on wave that he'd used on the Burmese crossing the border. He smiled, revealing a set of gold-capped incisors, and shouted something over his shoulder. A chunky individual with frayed shoulder boards bearing a couple of gilded pips appeared and snatched Shake's passport from the border guard. Apparently, an officer was required to deal with a roundeye.

The border police honcho jerked his head toward the little clapboard office under the ornate overhead span that marked the official border. "You...come." The officer hawked a gob and spit into the muddy Moei River running under their feet and led Shake into the office. There was a long counter fronting a rickety desk, and the honcho motioned for Shake to put his ruck on it. Shake did that and let the man dig through his meager belongings. The officer fiddled with a snarl of charger chords like he knew what he was seeing. He shook his head and made little *tsk tsk* scolding sounds when he found Shake's Kershaw folding knife. He snapped the knife open efficiently and ran a thumbnail along the partially serrated blade. "No good." He said making stabbing motions with the Kershaw. "You want, must pay."

While Shake was digging in his pocket, trying to strip a few bills rather than pull his money clip into view, the Border Police officer found the stash of videogames. The knife was promptly dropped back into his ruck and forgotten as the officer pawed through the selection, smiling, and pointing at a TV in the corner. Shake spotted wires leading to a videogame controller on the man's desk. He grabbed a copy of *Silver Surfer's Revenge* slapped another twenty on top of the game and handed it to the officer.

"For you."

"OK…OK…good…good." The Border Cop exhausted his English vocabulary and shoved Shake's pack across the counter with a wave at the door.

Shake walked into Thailand. There was a line of pedicabs waiting for passengers on the edge of Mae Sot. Shake climbed into one and told the driver to take him to the Irrawaddy Resort. As the driver pedaled behind him, Shake decided there were probably not enough videogames in the world to keep him out of jail if he got caught trying to slip a thirty-pound bar of pure gold into Burma on the return trip. Hopefully, Walt Ngo had a solution to that problem.

၁၁

Chris Anthony was pacing in the tiled entry to the Irrawaddy Resort when Shake arrived and leveraged his body out of the pedicab and paid his driver. They shook hands and walked through a lush tropical garden to Walter Ngo's room. Ngo was shouting into a phone, but he nodded and waved them toward a table full of ice buckets and drinks.

Shake dropped his jungle ruck and examined the drink display. There was an unopened bottle of Maker's Mark on the table and Shake reluctantly decided to leave it that way.

He poured some sort of carbonated fruit drink over ice before collapsing into a rattan chair. When Ngo finished his call, he shook hands and then walked to the drinks array where he sloshed scotch over an ice cube and sucked it down. "Christ, it's like herding cats!" He slumped into a chair and pulled a hard-sided camera bag from underneath it.

"Here you go," he said to Shake and used a foot to shove the bag across the tile floor. "Gold's there under a false bottom."

Shake opened the case and saw three lenses in preformed slots surrounded by a snarl of other photo accessories. He dug around a bit looking for a lift-tab or something that would let him take a look at the gold bar. Chris Anthony took the bag, secured the case cover, and turned it upside down.

"Only one way to access the hidden compartment," he said and dangled a thin brass plate suspended on a beaded chain. It looked something like a military dog tag with Lancer Technologies etched into the surface. "Works like this." Anthony lifted a section of the leather rim surrounding the bottom of the camera case and inserted the brass plate. With an audible click the bottom surface popped up about an inch. Anthony pulled it the rest of the way open to reveal the gold bar wrapped in a black velvet cloth.

Shake just ran a finger over the gold bar and nodded. Looked legit, just like the one he saw in Bangkok. He snapped the false bottom closed and hung the key around his neck. It was a little cheap and cheesy but likely to stand up under rudimentary inspection. He intended to avoid anything more detailed.

Walter Ngo handed over an envelope of paperwork. It was mostly financial statements. Shake recognized some of the outfits on the letterheads. There were read-outs on the world exchange value of pure gold from some very influential trading and financial firms.

"That should convince them we're offering what they're asking and more. If you have trouble convincing them, I'll be waiting on the other end of the phone to talk business. They've got the number."

"And you've got the rest in place?" Shake stuffed the financials back into the envelope and pocketed it.

Ngo stood and poured himself another drink. "We're working it now." He kept his back turned as he downed the drink. "You'd think I was trying to fence the fucking crown jewels or something."

"Relax, Walt." Chris Anthony stood and put a hand on his friend's shoulder. "We'll have the gold in place when they arrive at the border with Chesa and her sister." He retrieved another envelope from a messy desk in a corner of the room and handed it to Shake. It was full of currency.

"There's two grand in green; tens and twenties. Plus some Burmese *kyat*…which is mostly worthless paper. Use it as needed. Anything left when you get back is yours."

"Shit, Chris!" Walter Ngo slammed his glass on the desk. "The man is gonna get paid a lot more than that!"

"Of course he is…" Chris Anthony made placating gestures. "I was just…"

"Skip it…" Walt Ngo waved a hand and hit his drink. "Let me worry about that. Focus on getting the gold in place."

Anthony shrugged and pulled a map from the pile of paperwork. He showed Shake a spot he'd circled. "This will be the pick-up point. It's a clearing in a pineapple grove about a kilometer south of the little airport where you landed. We're gonna fly the gold in and move it to the clearing where they can pick it up." He handed over a mil spec GPS and punched some buttons. Waypoints out and back are programmed in. And when it's active, we can track you from here." Anthony gestured at an open laptop. "I presume you know how to use one of these?"

"Used 'em a time or two." Shake took the device and noted it was a generation advanced on the Blue Force Tracker system he'd used on active duty. Nothing imposing or too technical. Punch a button, it knows where you are. Punch another one and it tells you how to get where you've told it you're going. Batteries at full charge. Should last the trip, and he'd noted spares in the camera case. Navigation wasn't his primary concern anyway.

"You know…" Shake rattled the ice in his empty glass and Walt Ngo took it for a refill. "If that gold ain't where it's supposed to be when it's supposed to be, your wife and sister-in-law are in big trouble. A whole lot more than they're facing right now. Not to mention my old ass as the guy who's leading the parade."

"We'll have it there." Anthony folded the map and handed it over, giving Shake's shoulder a reassuring squeeze. "Don't worry about that."

Shake was worried. But not about money. In fact, he hadn't even thought about any kind of payday. Just doing something useful, something to keep a woman alive was about as deeply as he'd considered it. When you experience the pain of losing a woman you love, that's sufficient motivation to see the next guy doesn't have to go through it. Still the tension in the room was palpable and it made him uneasy. Maybe it was just fear and frustration. These dudes were not used to clandestine ops and doing things below legal radar.

It couldn't be easy to buy a million dollars' worth of pure gold. That had to set some red flags flying somewhere. And then get it quietly into Thailand past customs inspectors.

Finally, they had to fly it across a disputed border for pick up by an illicit anti-government lash-up. Some serious tension there, not to mention some serious legal problems if they got caught. And no matter how deep Walter Ngo's personal pockets might be, risking a million or more to ransom his wife from a gaggle of shady cutthroats was a big hit. No wonder they were a little goosey.

"Copy all." Shake shrugged off the uneasy feeling, drained his glass and stood. "I better get on the road. You said I was supposed to meet the guide here?"

ဂဂ

Pa Yet was smoking a hand-rolled smoke of tobacco that reeked like fumes from a chemical plant while sitting on the right front fender of a rusty, rump-sprung Land Rover Defender. When Shake, Chris Anthony, and Walt Ngo emerged from the Irrawaddy Resort blinking in the blazing sunshine, he jumped down and snapped into the position of attention. Shake eyed him carefully. The guy was obviously ex-military, staring grim-faced and motionless at the trio headed in his direction.

He was dressed in a well-worn khaki shirt handing loose over a pair of blue cargo trousers. The right leg of those trousers was bloused neatly over a scuffed Vietnam-era jungle boot. The left leg hung over what looked like a leather-wrapped ball, rounded at the ankle and flat on the bottom. Shake tried to avoid staring. Must be what's left of his foot and lower leg after the encounter with a mine.

Pa Yet bowed slightly when the introductions were made, but kept his dark eyes fixed on the man who was to be his passenger on the mission to Moulmein and back.

"Most happy meeting you," he said in fair English. His voice was raspy as if he was suffering from a sore throat, or too many hand-rolls. His sinewy nut-brown arms showed a few scars where they emerged from rolled up sleeves. Shrapnel. Shake had seen a lot of similar war souvenirs, carried a few on his own body. This guy saw some combat during his time in the Tatmadaw.

Shake eyed the Land Rover. It had experienced some rough terrain and a lot of muggy jungle atmosphere. There were rusted out spots all along the front and rear panels, but the tires looked fairly new. He noted a couple of spares strapped to the hood and roof of the vehicle plus three jerry-cans of what smelled like diesel.

"This thing gonna get us there and back?"

Pa Yet mirrored Shake's smile and gave the Rover an affectionate pat. A patch of rusty metal fell to the ground and Pa Yet kicked at it with his stump. "Not so good on outside. But I fix alla time. Plenty good inside." The driver-guide made a vague wave at the engine compartment. "Good road most of way to Moulmein." Shake was fairly sure the tough little bird hadn't read Kipling, but he was pleased to note Pa Yet used the old pronunciation. He was good to go.

Shake twirled a finger in the air. Pa Yet nodded at the familiar wind-it-up signal and crawled behind the wheel. The engine fired up with a healthy roar.

"How much does he know?" Shake walked a few steps back toward the hotel with Ngo and Anthony. "Practically everything," Walt Ngo said. "Like I told you before, he's real close to Chesa from his time in the hospital. He wants to help us get her back safely."

"So, he knows about the gold?"

"He knows it's on offer. We didn't tell him you were carrying a sample."

"Let's keep it that way—at least until I get a little better read on this guy."

"He's a good man, Shake." Walter Ngo gave Shake's shoulder another squeeze. "You can trust him."

"I damn sure hope so." Shake turned back to the idling Land Rover. "I'm gonna roll, gents. Call me on the sat phone as required. I'll do the same."

�’ာ

"I guess the first trick is to get us across the bridge," Shake said as he plopped the heavy camera case on the bench seat between them. "That gonna be a problem?"

"We use Number One Friendship Bridge." Pa Yet grinned and chuckled making the familiar finger-thumb rubbing sign for cash. "Man on duty pass us easy…show passport and twenny green. No problem." The driver seemed skilled, handling the Defender easily. The leather prosthetic didn't seem to present any problems as he clutched and shifted gears.

"You were a soldier." Shake lifted the top off a Styrofoam cooler at his feet and uncapped a water bottle. Pa Yet waved off an offer of water. He was busy rolling a smoke. Amazing dexterity. He rolled, licked, lit up, and shifted gears without missing a beat. "Tatmadaw ten years. Sergeant. Infantry scout." He hefted the leather-wrapped prosthetic up for Shake to examine. "Then this. Fooking mine…"

"Yep. Nasty business, Pa Yet."

"Please…you call me Pete. If OK by you?"

"Pete it is." Shake finished off his water and scrunched around to miss a coil spring that was jabbing him in the ass. "And you can call me Shake."

"Maybe so…" Pa Yet or Pete didn't seem comfortable with it. "Mistah Ngo say you officer?"

"Chief Warrant Officer when I retired, Pete, or what we call a Marine Gunner. But I was a regular soldier for many years before that."

"OK…Shek!" Shake's former enlisted status seemed to meet with Pete's approval. "Mistah Ngo say you were special sojer. Maline? Like John Wayne…Sand of Ima Jima?"

Shake laughed and shook his head. If The Duke only knew what a lasting legacy his role as Sergeant Stryker in that movie had on people all over the world. "I was a Marine, Pete. Maybe not so good as John Wayne but I got by." He waved a hand at the east. "Fought in a country over there."

"Veetnam…" Pete nodded impressed. "Platoon…Born on Four July…Firebase Gloria."

"Something like that." Shake wasn't a big war movie fan, but apparently his guide was. He had a feeling this road trip would involve some film reviews. Hopefully, Pete wouldn't want to hear a long series of war stories.

At the bridge checkpoint, Pete chatted with the familiar guard and passed over Shake's passport. The guard snatched the twenty without even looking at Shake's documents and waved them on across the bridge. They rumbled through downtown Myawaddy in a cloud of billowing dust until they reached the outskirts where Pete hung a left onto a paved road. A sign in several languages said they were rolling west on AH-1. Shake knew from the GPS in his lap that they had about 120 kilometers to cover before they reached Moulmein. He confirmed a waypoint on the electronics to let the folks on the other end know they were outbound. The Land Rover had no air conditioning, so he rolled down a stained and cracked window, sitting back to observe the verdant scenery rolling past. Couldn't have changed much since the days of World War II. Jungle was jungle. Had no age. It was literally a wall of vegetation from ground level up to a distant roof of vine-wrapped tropical trees.

No wonder Merrill and his Marauders limited their logistics support to air drops and mules. But it was hard to see how even a sure-footed mule, loaded with chow and ammo, could bull through this kind of bush. Shake's hands began to cramp as he remembered endless hours on the handle of a machete hacking through similar Vietnamese jungles. Chindits and Marauders. Had to be tough, determined dudes. He knew from personal experience the jungle was often more of an enemy than someone behind a rifle or machinegun waiting to kill you.

Shake needed distraction to chase away the haunts that he remembered from time in similar jungles. Sleep was out of the question on the roller-coaster ride provided by Pete's rattletrap Defender. If the vehicle had any shock absorbers when it was new, they were long gone and sorely missed on this trip. He watched the vegetation on the roadside, occasionally leaning away from a branch or bramble that sideswiped the vehicle. And he thought about mules.

According to the history he'd read and a few first-hand accounts from survivors, Merrill's columns depended on those rugged, long-suffering animals to help pack heavy weapons, chow, ammo, and water during their deep penetration forays against Japanese forces in Burma. Somehow General Frank Merrill had found among his volunteers some countryfied hard cases with experience as muleskinners. There was never much detail in those accounts. Shake wondered if Merrill's personnel experts combed the records to find men with mule-packing experience. Maybe among the people who showed up for service in Burma there was just naturally bound to be some roughnecks, teamsters, or farmers who learned stubborn endurance from mules and knew how to handle them.

Shake's grandfather, a farmer in Southeast Missouri who never seemed able to produce much of a cash crop, had four mules that he rented out to sharecroppers who couldn't afford a tractor. It was often young Shake's job to take a pair of Missouri mules to those farmers early each morning and pick up the weary animals at sunset. There was one lead jack—old Toby—who had a very cranky mind of his own. When Toby was tired, cantankerous, or just upset about something, he'd stop where he was and bray loudly. Nothing Shake tried, from tugging on a bridle to pleading for mercy by whispering into in one of Toby's long, twitchy ears, would get that mule moving when he wasn't in the mood to move. It was on one of Toby's stubborn days that Shake cut a hickory switch and applied it liberally to Toby's hindquarters. Who knew a mule could kick that high? Or hard enough to send a boy sliding down a dirt road on his ass with attendant abrasions and bruises?

It was a lesson well and painfully learned. That's the way of things with mules. And Shake was betting Frank Merrill and his Marauders must have had a Toby or two among the herd they used to pack themselves into jungle combat. Maybe when this was over, he'd do some research, write a little imaginative piece on that subject. Maybe call it something like *I was a muleskinner for Merrill's Marauders.*

છ૭

"They're on the highway and headed west." Chris Anthony looked up from his laptop.

Walter Ngo reached for his phone and hesitated as he slugged another hit of scotch. "I don't know, Chris. You sure we can trust these people you hired?"

"They're good for it. All ex-Thai Special Forces. And all well-paid, thus reliable. Stop obsessing and get us a progress report."

Walter Ngo paced the room as he talked on his mobile phone. It was mostly a one-sided conversation. He listened, nodding or grunting occasionally, as someone on the other end made a report. After a few minutes, he ended the call and retrieved his drink.

"OK. The stuff is inbound. They'll be here tonight."

"They brought the inflatables, right?"

"He said they've got everything they need." Ngo took a deep breath and checked his watch. "We're gonna have to prep it tonight or early tomorrow. You got the gilding stuff?"

"In the warehouse downtown. It'll work. We aren't dealing with precious metal experts here, Walt. I'm confident."

"Yeah..." Walter Ngo poured another shot of scotch over ice. "But it isn't your wife at risk, is it?"

၁၀၁

They hit the first Tatmadaw patrol just before tropical twilight. It was the time of day that movie people call magic hour when a setting sun casts pastel light at flat angles. Beautiful scene but the Burmese soldiers didn't look like they much gave a shit about tropical scenery. A squad of them lazed beside a makeshift barrier across the road. Most of them idled and smoked taking only an occasional disinterested glance at the approaching Land Rover. As Pete downshifted and slowed, one of them stood and raised a hand. They braked to a stop about twenty meters from the barrier.

The Tatmadaw troopers didn't look overly motivated or well-appointed, wearing a version of Chinese camo uniforms. Shake's trained eye went to the weapons they carried. Mostly what Major Semple told him he might see. What the Tatmadaw called BA-63 rifles for the most part, clone of the H&K G-3. The man approaching their vehicle sported shoulder boards and had a BA-93 Uzi clone hanging across his ammo rig.

"Sergeant…" Pete whispered. "You let me talk."

There was an exchange in Burmese during which Pete repeatedly pointed toward his passenger. The sergeant didn't seem overly impressed as he pulled a penlight and flashed it over Shake's smiling face. More Burmese and Shake followed Pete out of the vehicle. The sergeant waved at his troopers and a couple of them rose wearily to inspect the vehicle.

Shake reached inside his vest after the letter from the Cultural Minister and that caused the sergeant to swivel his subgun and shout an order. Shake locked his body with his hand buried inside the vest. He didn't understand the words, but he knew freeze-or-die when he heard it in any language.

"Pete, tell him I've got a letter from the government I want to show him." More conversation. "OK. He look." Pete smiled and motioned for the sergeant to relax as Shake slowly and carefully pulled the letter out of his pocket and handed it over.

The sergeant flashed his penlight and studied the document as his men rummaged in the back of the Defender. In his peripheral vision Shake saw two troopers pocketing bagged meals from their stash. They looked like kids pulling presents from under a Christmas tree. Shake decided not to make an issue of it. Hungry troopers will find chow. And the freeze-dried stuff had to be better than snake and lizard over rice.

There was more Burmese conversation and while the sergeant gabbed with Pete, Shake noted one of the search party pawing at his camera case. The man didn't lift it off the seat which likely would have forced Shake to explain why a collection of lenses and camera accessories weighed a damn ton.

"Letter OK." Pete ended the conversation and turned to Shake. "He say we must pay road tax."

And there's the shakedown. Shake smiled and nodded as if he was more than happy to pay this imaginary levy. "How much is this road tax?"

Pete shrugged and seemed to be counting the number of soldiers on roadblock duty. "You have Yew Ess dollah, Shek?"

"Yep. How many does he want?"

Pete flashed four fingers. "I think maybe forty green."

"Tell him OK…but I have to get it out of the truck." Shake edged slowly toward the vehicle and saw the sergeant's subgun muzzle following. "And Pete…try to keep him busy while I do it."

Burmese chatter. The sergeant nodded and swung the muzzle away from the Defender. Pete pulled his smoke makings out of a pocket and offered tobacco and papers to the NCO. The pair that had been rifling his gear saw the chance for a smoke break and walked over to join the party. Shake had the envelope full of cash in his pocket, but he didn't want to pull that wad out in front of the Tatmadaw. The road tax would have jumped considerably if they had a look at how much he was carrying.

While he rummaged around in his gear pretending to search for cash, he noted most of their packaged chow was gone along with some energy drinks and several bottles of water. Cheap at half the price. He palmed two twenties and returned to the roadblock.

The sergeant pocketed the money, handed back the intro letter and motioned for his men to remove the barriers. They were rolling again about an hour before local sundown. The GPS said they were a little less than halfway to their destination.

Pete engaged the four-wheel gearbox and steered the Defender into a left turn off the paved surface. They began jouncing over a narrow dirt road. The jungle on both sides seemed determined to squeeze the road closed and reclaim the intrusion. Somewhere up ahead, they'd have to find a clearing and camp for the night. He wanted plenty of daylight on the situation when they reached Moulmein.

The sat phone buzzed as Pete steered the vehicle around several large mangrove roots. Apparently, the patchy overhead foliage didn't interfere with the signal. Walt Ngo's voice came through loud and clear.

"We show you nearing the second waypoint. Everything OK?"

"Yeah…" Shake decided not to report the encounter with the Tatmadaw. Walt had enough problems. "We're rolling basically southwest. Looking for some place to spend the night. On to Moulmein at daybreak. We should be there around noon I figure. You good on your end?"

"Yeah, yeah. Working it twenty-four-seven. We'll be ready when you get back to the border." Ngo's tone was plaintive. It sounded like he was begging Shake to believe him.

"Got another call from the KNP. They gave us the meeting site. Chris is sending it through to your GPS. Looks like some kind of little complex on the outskirts of Moulmein. They'll be looking for you."

"Chesa and her sister OK?"

"I got a few seconds on the phone with her. Looks like they're treating them decently. Just anxious to get the hell out of there."

"I'm pretty anxious to make it happen. I'll check in again before we hit the meet site." Shake punched off the call and sat wondering if the gears of this giant jerry-rigged machine were beginning to mesh. Maybe he could pull this long-shot across the finish line if the KNP honchos bought into the gold deal. If they didn't just decide to go with a bird in hand, grab the single gold bar, disappear the hostages—and the messenger—and call it a day.

They rolled slowly through a couple of kilometers of rocky, potholed washboard. Shake's back suffered with every jolt and jerk. Pete seemed oblivious to it all. Rolling smokes and smiling in an amazing display of manual dexterity. He recounted what he remembered from a bunch of war movies, asking Shake's opinion about whether they were realistic or not. Since he'd not seen most of them, he didn't have much to say except a few comments about bottomless magazines and hand grenades that detonated with something resembling nuclear blasts. Pete agreed that movies about combat didn't match his experiences either. But he loved them anyway.

He changed subjects when they pulled over to refuel the Defender from one of the jerry-cans. "You think Missus Chesa OK?" It was the first time Shake had heard Pete mention her name. "Little bit worry…"

"Well, Pete. Mr. Ngo has talked to her. Seems she's OK." Shake strapped the empty fuel can into a shelf. "If everything goes right with the KNP, we'll get Chesa and her sister back into Thailand."

Pete fired up the diesel and grabbed a gear to get them back on the road. "Missus Chesa very strong woman, Shek. When they want to cut off my leg, she say no. I help her anyway I can."

"A lot depends on the KNP. You know much about them?"

"Very much hate military in Yangon. They call sojer officers in charge a…what's word? Joon Tah?"

"Junta, a bunch of people who will do anything to stay in power and control everyone else."

"Yes. KNP wants free from these people in Yangon. Lots of others want same but KNP very smart. Not just fight. KNP have plan."

"Well, they'll have a hell of a time against the Tatmadaw."

"They have idea to join all peoples who hate Yangon bosses. Fight Tatmadaw. Maybe kick out bosses in Yangon."

"They're about to get a bunch of money. You think they will stick to the deal?"

"KNP get gold become most powerful in Burma. Give some money, food, guns to other peoples. Want everyone to believe they are good people. Just fight for free of Yangon."

"Good people don't kidnap women and hold them for ransom. At least not where I come from…"

"In Myanmar is different, Shek. Take woman and sell for money OK if help in fight against Yangon Joon Tah."

"The end justifies the means…"

"We do what KNP bosses say. Missus Chesa be OK. That is most important thing." Pete pulled an amulet suspended on a chain from his sweaty shirt and rubbed it between his finger and thumb. "And we have Buddha and Nat."

"Buddha and what?"

"Nat…special spirit for Bamar people. Very much power."

"Well, stay on his good side, Pete. We'll take all the help we can get."

It was nearly dark and the Defender had only one working headlight that flickered with every bump in the road. Pete squinted into the gloom and pointed out the glow of lights in the distance. "Village. We get some eat and find camp."

Moei River, North of Mae Sot

T hree veteran Thai soldiers, all ex-Special Forces troopers with service in Pa Wai Airborne, stood waist-deep in the river loading bubble-wrapped bars into two Rigid-Hull Inflatable Boats. They'd been at it for the past two hours. A conga-line of porters passed the bars from a truck parked near the water. The RHIBs were nearly awash with their heavy loads.

"Tell them to be careful." Chris Anthony stood in ankle-deep mud flashing a hooded light on each bar as it passed. He pulled one of the porters aside and unwrapped the burden in the man's arms. "Some of it's not quite dry."

He rubbed a finger over the bar of gilded lead. His fingertip was smeared with gold paint. The gilded gloss with embedded gold flake was advertised as waterproof once it was dry, but they'd had to rush in triple-coating thirty-five lead ingots.

Walter Ngo stood nearby talking to the Thai officer in charge of the ex-soldiers. He was a stocky, muscular individual who seemed quite calm watching as his men labored in the dark. Walt eyed the man's black uniform, featureless except for the gaudy winged elephants flanking a parachute insignia on his left chest. "Your men know where to put this stuff?"

"Of course." The man shrugged as if he'd been asked a nettlesome question. "We conducted a recon last night and placed the wooden pallet in the clearing. All according to mission specs."

"Cut the bubble-wrap off and get rid of it once the bars are in place at the site. Just cover it with a poncho or something in case it rains. My wife and her sister should arrive the day after tomorrow. I'll call when we have a more specific time."

"We have been fully briefed by Mr. Anthony." The Thai officer didn't like being second-guessed by a shaky civilian. The bosses paid the fees, but they did not direct field operations. "And the weather will be clear for the next two days."

The Thai SF officer said something to one of his men and stepped away to watch a wooden box full of little black weapons being added to the load in one of the RHIBs. Ngo had seen enough TV shows to recognize submachine guns. Chris Anthony said they were suppressed H&K MP-5SDs, state of the special ops art in many circles. He also said the Thai former soldiers would use them expertly if anything went wrong at the exchange point across the river.

As the soldiers shoved the boats into the river and clambered aboard for the crossing into Myanmar, Walt Ngo prayed nothing would go wrong. If it did, Chesa and her sister might be caught in a crossfire. This whole stupid scheme might get her killed. It was a gamble he had to take. Chesa didn't know it—nobody knew it except Chris and his banker—but Walter Ngo was nearly broke and facing a vote of no confidence by the Lancer Technologies board of directors who were engineering a take-over from their absentee President and CEO. There'd been no time to liquidate what real assets he had remaining. The ruse had to work.

Village Northeast of Moulmein

By the bright standing lights under rusty China hats on the roadside, he could see that the village where Pete pulled over was really just a splay of little huts surrounding a ramshackle café/bar. He threw the heavy camera case over his shoulder for safekeeping and followed Pete toward the local watering hole.

Giant jungle moths making kamikaze runs on the lights causing flickering shadows as they ducked under a corrugated tin roof and looked around through a cloud of pungent tobacco smoke. Straight out of late chapters in Conrad's Heart of Darkness. All rattan and bamboo with some rickety card tables wobbling on an uneven dirt floor.

The joint was fairly crowded with characters that likely melted out of the jungle at sunset. Drawn here like moths because it was a spot of light in the darkness. And there was no place else to go if you were hungry or thirsty and had a few *kyat* to spare. The customers were mostly sun scorched men wrapped waist-down in tube-like sarongs over bare feet or plastic sandals. Most of them were laid way back, using greasy fingers to inhale some sort of rice-based chow or sucking on typhoon jugs of local beer.

Exotic, decrepit, reeking of jungle ambiance, Kipling would have loved this place. Shake snapped some photos as Pete led them to a table and the camera caused a few customers to shy away, turning backs to a roundeye tourist with no manners. A few of them had machetes strapped by braided cord at the waist. Shake noted the finely-honed edges and put the camera into the case on top of the gold.

They ordered beer which arrived lukewarm, brought to their table by a slender woman with face and arms painted in rudimentary designs. The beer had a fishy smell and a vinegary taste.

Shake swallowed it wishing he could find a good drink of bourbon whiskey somewhere. He tried not to miss it, but there were times when he really thirsted for the bite and burn of good whiskey. Bad whiskey in a pinch. Chan was always on him about it, wondering why he couldn't seem to sit still reading a book or watching TV without a healthy slug at his elbow. He used to think of it as his demon chaser. Sometimes it worked but not always. Shake's demons were sly bastards.

He shook it off and looked around the room, smiling at the serving woman and several others wearing differing designs in the elaborate native makeup. "*Thanaka.*" Shake nudged Pete and pointed. "Saves very much on lipstick."

"You know *thanaka*? Very good, Shek!" Pete hit his beer, stood, and ducked under the overhang. He was back in moments carrying a long sliver of wood. "Made from this. Outside of tree." He made grinding motions. "Woman put this, little water, make paste…*thanaka!*"

Pete ordered food and then spent some time sketching various designs with vague explanations about their meaning. What it boiled down to was personal taste in skin art. Didn't have to mean anything. Much like the tattoos so popular in the States. If you saw a design you liked, you just had it inked into your skin or in Burma painted on your face and hands. Kipling would have been disappointed that there wasn't something more arcane and mysterious about it.

The menu was limited to what the proprietor had on hand which in their case was fish sauce over rice noodles, a dish Pete called *mohinga*. It was spicy enough to break a sweat but otherwise quite tasty as was a salad called *lahpet* made from green tea leaves.

They ate in silence, listening to pleasant gabble from nearby tables. Every so often there was a shout or laugh from a guy seated nearby who seemed to be enormously enjoying his own company. The guy was some kind of official, maybe a cop, and about three typhoon jugs beyond any kind of sobriety. He was dressed in bush-stained grey shirt and trousers that looked uniform. Shake couldn't identify any sort of insignia, but he immediately spotted a 1911 or clone hanging loosely in a canvas holster at the man's waist.

"Who's the comedian?" Shake nodded at the man who now plopped mud-caked jungle boots on a table and drained his beer bottle.

"*Ka Kwe Ya.*" Pete leaned across his plate and whispered. "You call local army…peoples' militia?"

"Is there a milia outfit around here?"

Pete didn't think so. He expected the happy man was probably on leave from an outfit elsewhere in the countryside. Major Semple said there were a lot of local militias in Burma, some loosely sponsored by the Tatmadaw, some on the other side of the fence and classified as EAO, or Ethnic Armed Organizations. Shake recalled the Regional or Popular Forces he knew from his service in Vietnam. Those guys were the Rodney Dangerfield's of the war. No respect—and very little pay or support.

"Let's buy him a beer."

The militia man gave them a gap-toothed smile and slid into a chair. When Pete offered some of the *mohinga* left on his plate, the guy scooped up the remnants like he hadn't eaten for a day or two. Shake grinned and eyed the pistol. It looked old but not very shot-worn. The militiaman was happy to let him take a closer look for another jug of beer.

The pistol was a very old Colt original. A first-generation M1911 before the modifications that turned the sidearm into an 1911A1. Much of the original bluing was gone, but the exposed bare metal was clean of rust with only a few visible pits. The bore was shiny, and it looked like the lands and grooves would still spin a bullet adequately. It was a collector's item in most parts of the gun-owning world. Shake had Pete negotiate and bought the pistol plus 10 rounds of 230 grain ball ammo for another beer and twenty green.

ဿ

Shake brewed coffee over a small fire at a roadside clearing while Pete worked under a flashlight to get his second headlight operating. A couple of flashes in the dark indicated he'd succeeded. Pete approached wiping his hands and pocketing a screwdriver. "Lights fix now." He held up a roll of duct tape. "Can fix anything you have this."

"There it is." Shake handed over a cup of coffee. "Without duct tape this mundane sphere of ours would be barren, bleak, and dank." Pete shrugged and sipped his coffee. Shake offered him a pinch of Copenhagen wintergreen. The driver sucked on it for a while, then spit it out and rolled one of his redolent smokes.

Pete stared down at his fake foot. It looked more like a giant paw, like pictures he'd seen of elephants or rhinos—a big flat paw minus the toes. It worked well enough and allowed him to stump along without too much of a limp. He was lucky to be alive after triggering the ambush on that day nearly two years ago.

They had been sent to find the camp of some sort of armed rebel outfit operating close to the Thai border. No one really knew what kind of rebels. There was a long list of them on the Tatmadaw's roster of Ethnic Armed Organizations. Could be any or all of them. Pete didn't know, and it wasn't his mission that day to find out more than where they were. He led a four-man deep reconnaissance team along the base of a jungle covered hill. Normally, he'd be up on the high ground and observe from there, overlooking the trail where there was evidence of recent heavy foot traffic. But it had been a tough and fruitless slog for the past three days, and Pete was tired. The trail was easier going and intersected a road that led to Mae Sot. When he reached the road, he reached the limit of his recon route. If he didn't spot the rebels before the road, he'd have to turn back and re-run the mission in the other direction.

His feet, stuffed into a pair of decrepit boots that were at least a size too small, were aching something fierce, and Pete decided he'd pause somewhere before they hit the road and cut the toes out of his boots. He was unlikely to get a new pair anytime soon, but he couldn't go much farther on cramped and blistered feet. He stepped to the edge of the trail, holding up a clenched fist to signal a halt and turned to see his three followers take a knee. That's when it happened.

He couldn't remember if it was a tripwire or the actual mine detonator that he stepped on. All he remembered was a bright flash and being hurled through the air into the surrounding bush. As he lay gasping in pain, he heard the rattle of AKs firing on full auto and realized they'd walked into an ambush. Enemy on the high ground were cutting into his patrol. Exposed on the trail, they never had a chance. It must have been what they called a "toe-popper," a low-order explosive detonation, but it was effective. Dragging his mangled left leg, he managed to crawl off into a stand of bamboo, fighting the pain and listening to the rebels put kill shots into his men. He waited for them to come for him, but it was quiet after the desultory finishing shots. The rebels likely thought the soldier who tripped the mine must be dead. They didn't bother looking for him, and that gave him enough time to assess the damage to his leg. It was a bloody mess. He could see bone and muscle showing below his knee, and the mangled limb was pumping blood. He had to stop the bleeding. He needed a tourniquet.

In the cargo pocket of his trousers, Pete felt for the roll of duct tape he always carried to make equipment repairs in the field. He'd been planning to repair his boots with it once he cut the toes open, but he had more serious problems just then. He wrapped the tape tightly around his left leg just above the damaged part and below his knee. In a few minutes the blood flow ceased to a trickle. He waited some time to be sure the rebels had departed and then began to crawl toward the road.

A trucker on the way to Mae Sot spotted him, loaded Pete into the back of a flat-bed, and sped for help at the nearest medical facility—the refugee camp where the trucker knew doctors and nurses treated sick or injured people on both sides of the river. He was fading in and out of consciousness when they carried him into the little hospital. He didn't remember much beyond some kind of argument between a doctor and a woman about how to treat his wounds. He discovered later that the woman was Chesa Ngo and she was pleading with the doctor to save his knee. If they could save the knee, he might walk again, limping but upright on what was left of his own limbs.

He got to know Chesa Ngo well as he lay in the camp recovering after the amputation of his left leg below the knee. She was a very special lady, he discovered, a Karen like himself, who volunteered to help people here at Mae Sot. She was married to a rich American who helped by spending a lot of money in and around the refugee camps. Some of her husband's money went into crafting an artificial lower leg for him. Chesa worked with him for weeks until the stump was strong enough to support his weight. She hired a shoemaker to build the artificial calf and foot and helped him learn to walk again by supporting him as he slowly got used to taking his weight on the improvised foot. Chesa was a special woman who promised someday she'd bring in a specialist from America who would fit him with a better prosthetic.

It was during his recovery that he decided not to return to the Tatmadaw. He had no living family. After a time in an orphanage, he'd joined the Tatmadaw mainly to eat and earn a living on what pittance military service paid. And the Tatmadaw made no special provisions to support wounded men. A little money maybe, but then they were cut loose to beg or steal for a living.

Like many other soldiers caught up in miliary operations in his turbulent home country, Pete was simply listed as missing in action and presumed dead. His command had likely long since written him off, just another low-level NCO dead at the hands of rebels. Not unusual and no big deal in the corrupt Tatmadaw. No one from the Border Police or the army units based around Mae Sot knew him personally.

After a few months learning to walk, he began to do chores and errands for Chesa and the hospital staff. She was so kind and generous, even put up the money to help him buy a well-used Land Rover that gradually became the hospital's delivery truck. Pete learned to drive the truck and roamed everywhere along the border, picking up refugees that needed treatment and ferrying supplies up from Bangkok. He had a new life. He could walk and drive. All that was thanks to Chesa Ngo. He owed her a lot.

"Shek…" Pete sucked on his cigarette and squinted into the dark jungle surrounding their camp. "You think KNP OK for gold? Not want Yew Ess dollah?"

Shake thought about it and decided he'd seen enough to trust the old Tatmadaw vet. "Let me show you something." He pulled the camera case into the firelight and keyed open the false bottom. "Take a look at this."

Pete scrunched around until he could see firelight reflecting off the gold bar. "Sunnabeech…" He poked at the bar like he expected it to bite back and whispered in reverent tones. "I never see before."

"That's gold, Pete…pure-dee-fucking gold." Pete's mouth hung open and his eyes were saucer size. "This little bar is just to get their interest. Mr. Ngo will have a bunch more of it waiting for the KNP when we get back to Myawaddy with Mrs. Ngo and her sister."

"I think KNP shit pants." He laughed and patted the gold bar. "Nobody Burma have this. Missus Ngo be OK."

It wasn't a very comfortable night. Pete spent it curled up on the back seat of the Defender with windows rolled up against hordes of mosquitos that appeared like an 8th Air Force Bomb Group around midnight. Shake slathered himself with DEET and slung his old jungle hammock between two hardwoods just off the road. The woven net cocoon was a tight squeeze between his bulk, the pistol, and the camera case, but he'd spent nights in worse accommodations.

Shake drifted off looking up through the jungle overhang at a bright white moon and thinking about his wife. Chan would have loved to be here with him. Her curious nature and enthusiasm for exploring was part of why he loved her so much. She was fascinated by weird situations and quirky characters. And this trip was damn sure chock full of both.

He wanted to be up and on the road at dawn, so his internal alarm clock was nudging him awake just as the first fingers of sunlight penetrated the jungle gloom. He rolled over setting the hammock swinging and that saved his life. He heard something rustling nearby and then a loud thwack as a blade bit through his hammock suspension line just above his head and dumped him on the ground.

The next thing he heard was a loud boom as someone fired what sounded like a small howitzer over near the parked Defender. As Shake rolled, scrambling to find his new pistol, he saw a dark little man in a ratty shirt and khaki shorts dancing around as he worked to lever the machete out of the hardwood. Sporting a matted and tangled afro, he looked like a deranged heavy-metal fan and smelled like an open sewer. Sinewy arms and legs covered with weeping jungle sores.

Shake located the pistol. There was a round in the chamber, but he racked the slide anyway, hoping the sound would register with the man on the business end of the machete. Looked like a teenager, maybe even younger and Shake didn't want to blow him away unless it was absolutely necessary.

He shouted and pointed the pistol, but the kid didn't turn until there was a second loud boom from the direction of the Land Rover. That got his attention. Shake cut a quick glance over his left shoulder and saw a smoking gun barrel being pulled back inside the vehicle. He looked back to pick up his pistol sights just as the teenager freed his machete and charged with a banshee screech.

The kid was right-handed and that allowed Shake to spin left toward his gun hand and dodge the first swipe. The attacker was no streetfighter, swinging too hard, off balance and not ready for any kind of follow-up as Shake thumped him hard at the base of the skull with the pistol barrel. When he went down to his knees, still screeching like a banshee, Shake aimed the .45 for a shot to the temple. *Do I really want to scatter this kid's brains all over the jungle? Would a plea of self-defense hold legal water in Burma?* Even if it did, the arrest and investigation would blow his mission deadlines.

He'd just about decided to let it rest when the kid rolled and swiped the machete way too close to Shake's gut. *That's the way you want to play this? Your call.* Wishing he'd test-fired the old pistol, Shake pressed the trigger. The Colt barked and bucked sending a round center mass in the kid's heaving chest. Thank you, Mr. Browning. The heavy .45 round smacked into the kid's breastbone and dumped him straight backwards. He spasmed and gasped a couple of times and then lay still pumping blood from the exit wound into the jungle floor.

Pete crawled out of the Defender and came trotting up with a short double-barrel shotgun hanging from his right hand. It looked like an old hammer-fired, double-trigger coach gun with a stubby barrel and rounded stock cut down to pistol size. He barely glanced at the dead kid on the ground who was already drawing a black blanket of flies.

"OK, Shek?"

"I'm good, Pete. Who the hell are these guys?"

Pete nudged a scabrous arm with his stump and pointed at the kid's gaping mouth. Most of the teeth missing and purple gums. "*Ya ba*…they want money for more."

"What the hell is *ya ba*?" But Shake had it figured from what Major Semple told him about the proliferation of meth-amphetamine labs in the Burmese jungle.

"Very bad drug." Pete made little stabbing motions at his forearm. "Young man work for *ya ba* maker. Smuggle *ya ba* into Thailand. Sometime take sample. Need more alla time."

He shrugged and broke open the coach gun to reload. "Then this."

Pete led the way back toward the Defender and pointed at a second man lying nearby. Same look, same scab-covered arms and legs. And a gaping fly-blown hole where one of Pete's 12-gauge buckshot rounds tore through his gut.

"What now?" He half expected a flood of Burmese cops or a squad of Tatmadaw to emerge with crime-scene tape and flashing lights.

"No problem." Pete just shrugged and pointed at the jungle along the roadside. They carried the dead meth-heads into the jungle and dumped them. There was a pick-mattock and shovel strapped on the Defender. Shake was about to retrieve them and dig a couple of shallow graves, but Pete waved off the idea. "No need. Maybe tiger eat good tonight."

They left the dead men and walked back to police up their camp site and reload the Defender for the last leg of the trip to Moulmein. Shake figured to arrive sometime around noon or shortly thereafter. "Better to hide guns." Pete pulled out a section of floorboard on the passenger side of the vehicle. "No good have guns when we get to Moulmein." He slotted the shotgun into a hidden compartment and held out a hand for Shake's pistol.

Shake slumped into his seat as Pete fired up the engine and steered them back onto the road. He tried to tamp the adrenaline rush as dawn broke over the treetops. Hard to comprehend. West meets east and junkies everywhere. They'd damn near been killed by a couple of meth-heads deep in the Burmese jungle.

Moulmein

Just after a skimpy morning meal, one of the female guards pulled Chesa aside and escorted her to a meeting with Pha Pat. She found herself in a dimly lit room where rattan ceiling fans whirled overhead barely moving the muggy air. An array of electronics on a long mahogany table—a couple of laptops and three or four mobile phones—made her think it was some sort of KNP command center.

Seated at the table were Pha Pat and an older man in native dress. Miyat Win? The man she'd seen talking to Endra. Pha Pat motioned for Chesa to take one of the chairs on the opposite side of the table. As she sat, she noticed one-eyed Pak standing in a dark corner with a rifle strapped across his chest. He was the only one not smiling.

"We have very good news." Pha Pat pointed at one of the cell phones on the table. "Your husband's representative will arrive today." He checked a gold watch on his left wrist. "In a few hours I should think."

"And then this will be over?" Chesa waved a hand around the room. "You will let us go?"

"Much depends on your husband's representative." Pha Pat sounded like a schoolteacher lecturing backward students. "If your husband has met our demands and there is no nonsense, you will be free to return with him to the border. If not…" Pha Pat cut a glance at one-eyed Pak. "Well, we are prepared to exercise our options."

"There is one issue…" Miyat Win leaned forward with his elbows on the table. "Your sister Endra…"

"What about her?"

"We have been talking. She understands our struggle. Much better than you do, I think. It is possible that your sister may wish to stay behind, to stay with us and help our cause."

"No!" Chesa jumped to her feet. "She is just a child. She has no idea what she wants. I'm her older sister, she will do as I say. Endra will return with me to Thailand!"

"Despite what you think…" Miyat Win used a finger to shove his spectacles higher on his nose. "We are not criminals. We are forced by circumstances in this country to sometimes take harsh measures. But we respect each person's right to choose a path in this life. We will not force your sister to stay with us. On the other hand, if Endra chooses to stay, we will not force her to leave."

"I will speak to her. Endra will leave with me."

Miyat Win shrugged and sat back in chair. "We will see what path your sister chooses when the time comes."

"In the meantime," Pha Pat picked up one of the phones that was vibrating on the table. "You must prepare yourself for a journey if that path is open to you and your sister."

He waved a hand. Meeting concluded. One of the female guards stepped up to lead her from the room. She saw one-eyed Pak step forward and bend close to Pha Pat for whispered instructions.

ೲ

Endra was flirting shamelessly with a young man in the hallway outside their room when Chesa arrived from her meeting. She was giggling, doing a little hip-swiveling dance before the wide-eyes of one of the interior guards who sometimes refilled the water jars in their room. The man was a teenager, maybe a year or two older than Endra, and Chesa had run him off several times over Endra's objections.

"Get in the room!" Chesa grabbed her sister by an elbow. "They are coming to rescue us. We must pack."

Endra pouted but allowed herself to be dragged away from her boyfriend. "Pack?" She flounced in the baggy dress that they were issued. "We have nothing. There is nothing to pack." Chesa glared at the grinning guard and shoved her sister inside their room.

"I was just told that you have spoken about staying here with these people, the KNP. I forbid it!"

Endra collapsed on her sleeping pallet and covered her eyes with the back of a hand. "I'm old enough to have my own life, Chesa. You are not my mother!"

"I am your elder sister. And you will obey me!"

"The KNP fights to make all Bamar people free of the Yangon junta. They need people to help, to fight for freedom."

"They will do that without you, Endra. You are not a soldier. You would wind up cleaning and sweeping! And carrying some idiot's child! You will go with me to America. You will get an education as I did."

"You just think you are so much better than everyone else, Chesa! Just because you married a rich American…"

"I married the man I love, the man who will get us out of this mess. Now stop arguing. We must bathe and prepare to leave."

၇၀၃

"We're here." Shake sat with the sat phone pressed to his ear, looking down from a little rise at what must be the KNP compound. The GPS said so and he could see walls plus a gate topped with coils of razor wire.

He could also see the famous Moulmein pagoda in the distance, sticking up over the nearby town like a gilded globe with a long slender spire pointed at the sky. Love to visit, Rudyard, maybe see the sun come up like thunder out of China across the bay. Maybe next time.

"OK, you should be set." Walt Ngo sounded tense but encouraging. "We told them you'd show in a beat-up Land Rover. They're expecting a Mister Davis and translator. Remember, if you hit a snag, call me."

"OK…but I'm guessing the first thing these guys will do is grab my phone and the GPS. It's what I'd do."

"No matter, Shake. We've been talking to them on their phone. We'll be able to stay in touch."

"Copy…" He looked over at Pete and shrugged. "We're rolling…time now."

"One last thing…" Walt Ngo shouted into his ear. "When you see Chesa, tell her not to worry. No matter what happens, tell her I love her."

No matter what happens? What happens damn sure better be what's called for in the plan. If not, some dangerous defecation might hit the oscillation. But cross that bridge if and when encountered.

Shake pulled his cash and passport and stuffed them under a section of the Defender's dashboard. Then he stuffed the slim five-inch Kershaw folder deep into his boot top and rolled his sock over it. Should feel like just part of a thick ankle if a guy was doing a superficial frisk. He flicked a finger at the windscreen and Pete drove them down the hill toward the KNP compound.

They braked in a cloud of dust and Shake sat for a moment going over his pitch about the gold and patting his pockets for the support documents. He nodded to Pete, shouldered the camera case, and climbed out to stand in the brutal sun. The gate swung open and three armed men emerged cautiously behind aging M-16s hanging from frayed slings. All three muzzles were pointed straight at him.

The lead man was a tall, rangy guy with a snakeskin wrap around a mop of unruly black hair. Looked like what was left of a large Burmese snake or lizard. One side of the skin was pulled down pirate-style to cover the man's left eye. Shake noticed a long slash of pale scar tissue above and below the patch. Ugly dude. Mr. Cyclops was muscle not brains. Likely brains were waiting inside the compound.

Burmese chatter. Cyclops barking and Pete responding calmly. "He want to know who we are."

"Did you tell him?"

"Yes…" The three goons approached. "They want to search." Shake placed the camera case at his feet and raised his hands.

As expected, they found the sat phone and GPS almost immediately. Cyclops dropped both into a little haversack hanging from his hip. The rest of the pat-down was cursory, amateur hour. Overly excited about finding the phone and GPS. They missed the Kershaw folder completely. Shake made no objection to losing the electronics. Hopefully, the bosses would have the stuff returned before these clowns could hawk them on the black market.

When the body search was complete, Cyclops jabbed at Shake's camera case with the muzzle of his rifle. "Tell him to leave it, Pete. It's for his bosses inside."

Pete tried but the one-eyed goon was having no part of it. He motioned to one of his men and the goon began to open the buckled lid. Shake bent to retrieve the case and found an M-16 muzzle under his chin.

"He say you back up…" Pete chatted away in Burmese but Cyclops ignored him and took his own look at the gear inside the case. He pawed around a bit and then hefted the case by its neck strap, firing a question in Pete's direction. "He ask why so heavy, Shek. Think maybe bomb inside."

"Tell him there ain't no fucking bomb inside, Pete. Tell him what's inside is for his bosses…and his bosses only." More Burmese chatter but Cyclops wasn't convinced or appeased. He batted the case with the muzzle of his rifle and then gave it a resounding kick.

"Jesus Christ…" Shake shook his head. If it was a bomb this idiot would set it off right here. Last thing he wanted to do was show this low-level dipshit a bar of pure gold. He made placating gestures at Cyclops. "Just tell him to wait…"

There was a quiet command from someone standing just inside the open gate. Whoever it was had some influence. Cyclops and his buddies backed off, motioning for Shake and Pete to head for the gate. Shake retrieved the camera case and walked toward the compound. On the other side of the wall was a squatty two-story concrete building. Not much to it. Maybe some sort of Chinese or Russian no-frills prefab. He noticed a small bald man entering the building with a cell phone pressed to his ear. Brains, the man in charge. But the bald guy disappeared behind a heavy entry door before Shake could say anything to him.

Two guards pinned them up against a concrete wall like a couple of low-level perps as Cyclops disappeared through a door just off the main corridor and slammed it shut behind him. They put sweaty backs against the wall and waited for whatever was going to happen next.

Cyclops appeared after about 15 minutes and motioned for Shake to follow him inside. Pete began to follow but the guards stopped him. "He goes with me." Shake halted and pointed at Pete. "He's the translator." Pete explained in Burmese and Cyclops barked back at him. "He say no need. Men inside speak English."

That was confirmed as Shake entered a muggy little office space lit by dim overhead bulbs that swayed in the breeze from a ceiling fan.

"You are Mister Davis."

It was a statement, not a question, so Shake just nodded and looked around the office space as Cyclops peeled off behind two men seated at a long mahogany table. The speaker was the bald guy who called off the dogs outside. Next to him was a smaller man in native dress. Big Boss and Little Boss. The KNP brain trust.

Big Boss motioned for Shake to approach. He walked forward with the camera case cradled in his arms, eyeing a litter of electronics on the table. These guys were wired. His sat phone and GPS were piled next to an Apple laptop. The little half-chewed apple logo glowed in the gloom.

"You are a representative of Mister Walter Ngo, President of Lancer Technologies." Again, a statement rather than a question so Shake just nodded. "And you have the money required for the release of Chesa Ngo and her sister?" That one was definitely a question. The two boss men were eyeing him curiously. Probably wondering which of his pockets contained a million dollars in small denominations.

"About that…" Shake plopped the camera case down on the table. "Mr. Ngo has sent me with something I think you'll find more valuable than U.S. dollars."

Cyclops leveled his rifle at him as Shake pulled the little brass plate out from under his shirt and upended the case. Little Boss waved away the muzzle but both men leaned cautiously back in their chairs. "Mr. Ngo wants to meet your demands. He knows that you might have problems with U.S.

currency here in Myanmar…government problems, exchange rates and the like." Shake inserted the brass plate under the lining. "So, he's offering this." The false bottom gave way with a click. Shake lifted it and pulled the velveteen cloth away from the gold bar. Both bosses stood and examined the gold. Shake lifted it out of the case and carefully arranged it to catch some of the dim overhead light.

"What you have here…" Shake tapped the bar and ran a finger over the etching on the surface. "…is pure gold, the most valuable commodity in international markets worldwide." He watched the bosses who simply stared wide-eyed and launched into his prepared pitch. "You might have troubles with currency which has variable exchange rates and sometimes can't be used in trade for one reason or another. With gold, you won't have that kind of worry. Everyone wants gold and everyone recognizes its stability in worldwide markets."

Little Boss hefted the gold bar and seemed amazed at its weight. Big Boss produced a small knife and scratched at it, leaving a small groove in the surface right under the etching that proclaimed the bar 999.9 pure gold. He rubbed the little sliver he'd carved out between a thumb and finger. Both bosses slowly refolded themselves into their seats. Cyclops stood slack-jawed staring at the gold bar on the table. Clearly not what these dudes expected. And likely something they'd never seen before.

"We requested…demanded…" Little Boss kept rubbing a hand across the gold bar. "Mr. Ngo agreed to one million dollars…but this…"

"This…" Shake rapped the gold with his knuckles. "This gold bar right here is worth about sixty-five thousand U.S. dollars today." He pulled the documents from his pocket and spread them on the table and launched into some of the dialogue he'd memorized. "The important thing is that unlike paper money, gold never loses value. Market prices might fluctuate a bit, but the trends are up, not down as you can see from these documents prepared by some very reliable market analysts."

He took a deep breath, licking at a rivulet of sweat that was running down his face, and watched as the bosses examined the documents. Little Boss seemed to know something more about what they said than Big Boss. There was a rapid-fire exchange in Burmese.

"This is not enough." Little Boss neatly stacked the documents. Big Boss kept his eyes on the gold bar. "We require one million dollars. That is not negotiable regardless of the medium of exchange." Shake nodded. Little Boss was the bigger brain here. Shake sat in the nearby rattan chair uninvited and crossed his legs.

"Mister Ngo agrees to your terms. This is just what we'd call earnest money. He wanted you to see that he's cooperating…in fact, he's offering more than you're asking if you factor in market values for gold."

"This is not one million dollars…" Big Boss finally took his hand off the gold bar and reached for a teacup near his elbow. "This is not the deal we made with Mister Ngo."

"As I said…" Shake reached for a bottle of water and got a nod from Little Boss. He unscrewed the cap and took a drink. "This is just to show you that Mister Ngo intends to meet your price in gold. The rest of it is waiting for you to pick it up at a location near the border."

"He has one million dollars in gold stored near the border with Thailand?" Big Boss sounded like he couldn't believe that. Little Boss was looking at the paperwork, calculator running in his head.

"That's correct, gentlemen." Shake hoped he sounded like a veteran businessman negotiating a deal. He felt like he was operating out of his MOS and way above his paygrade. "And by the time you arrive to claim it…" Shake pointed at the paperwork. "…that gold will likely be worth much more than one million dollars on the world market." Shake took another drink of water, watching the KNP bosses carefully. Might just have pulled this off. Little Boss is on board. Big Boss is hesitant but leaning.

"So, here's what we propose. We take a trip up to Myawaddy with Mrs. Ngo and her sister. You get the gold, no questions asked. I take the two women across into Thailand and our business is complete."

"This is not what we expected, Mr. Davis." Big Boss was blustering. "How do we know we can trust this arrangement?"

"You can make a call." Shake pointed at the pile of phones. "Speak to Mister Ngo directly. He's just across the border in Thailand. And he's not going to do anything stupid. Not with his wife and her sister at risk. He's got the gold in place for you." He nodded at his GPS "I've got the exact location."

"We must consider…" Little Boss was chewing on the problem. Big Boss reached for one of the phones. "You will wait outside." He flicked a hand at Cyclops. "Pak will see that you and your driver have some food and drink."

"Before we go any further…" Shake stood and watched Cyclops rounding the table. "I want to see Mrs. Ngo and her sister."

"They are fine, Mr. Davis. They have been well treated."

"I'll just take a look for myself."

Cyclops got his orders and led Shake out of the little KNP command post. Pete was in a chair near the door. He and the two guards were shrouded in smoke from his hand-rolls. "Let's go, Pete." Shake waved and followed Cyclops down the corridor. "Let's take a look and see how Mrs. Ngo is doing."

Cyclops led them to the end of the corridor past one open space that was clearly a kitchen and another that looked like a tiled bathing area. There were several other doors along the way, but they were all shut. Cyclops shoved Shake and Pete into a small room and said something to a female inside. She eyed the strangers suspiciously and then walked out. Keeping his rifle pointed, Cyclops retreated to a dark corner.

Shake wandered to a window and stared out into the late afternoon sun that glinted off the Moulmein Pagoda in the distance. Got to be tourists with a literary bent or diehard Kipling fans visiting the area. People would have to notice armed men wandering around nearby. Either the good folks of Moulmein didn't know about the KNP headquarters, or they weren't concerned. There must be some kind of police or military presence in a town like this one located on a little finger inlet off the Andaman Sea, but no sign of any sort of interest in a nearby rebel compound. Peaceful coexistence or serious bribe money changing hands. At this point in his experience with Burma, he'd believe either one.

The door opened and the female guard waved Chesa Ngo and her sister into the room. They were dressed in drab, baggy cotton shifts that hid their body shape, but both seemed healthy and unharmed. Chesa was an exotic beauty with dark almond-shape eyes, long glossy black hair, and an olive cast to her skin. Made sense in that moment why Walt Ngo would cough up a million in gold to have her back safe and sound. She smiled brightly and rushed to hug Pete. Sister Endra, a teenage clone of her older sister, stood her ground and pouted.

"Mrs. Ngo…" Shake walked over and smiled. "My name is Davis. Your husband sent me to escort you back to Thailand. Please call me Shake."

She shook hands. Firm grip and beaming smile showing a brace of fine white teeth. "I am so glad to meet you, Mr. Davis…Shake." She pointed at her sister. "This is Endra." The younger sister might have smiled but it looked more like a painful grimace. "When can we leave?"

"That depends on the KNP fellows down the hall." Shake walked over to shake hands with Endra. She passed on that and gave Shake a little bow over folded hands. "I believe they're talking to your husband right now. Should be no problem. Probably leave here shortly for Myawaddy."

"We go in my truck, Missus Chesa." Pete was like a kid seeing his Mom after a long separation. "You remember my truck?"

"Is that thing still running?" She laughed and pointed at his prosthetic. "And you learned to use the pedals?"

Pete stomped on his stump and did a little happy dance. "Everything fine, Missus Chesa. We go home soon."

A phone buzzed and Cyclops jammed it to his ear. A few grunts and he motioned for Shake and Pete to follow him out of the room. "We come back soon." Pete shouted as they were herded out the door. "Don't worry…be happy."

Shake caught Chesa Ngo's eye. "Your husband said to let you know he loves you." She seemed almost ready to cry despite the smile on her face. Shake nodded and smiled. "But I expect you know that."

Big Boss met them halfway down the corridor. "We have spoken to Mr. Ngo. And we have tentatively accepted his proposal. Provided all goes as promised, we will release Mrs. Ngo and her sister at Myawaddy." And return with a shit-pot full of gold to become kings of the Burma tribal resistance.

Shake thought it but kept silent. Up the rebels. If these back-bush clowns use all that gold to clean house in Rangoon the country would be better off for it.

"Great…" Shake checked his watch. "When can we get on the road?"

"There are logistic concerns, Mr. Davis. We will stay off the main roads which means a longer trip than usual. You will remain here overnight. We will depart for Myawaddy early in the morning."

"Your call, I guess. But I want my phone back so I can report to Mr. Ngo."

"We have discussed all this with him."

"Listen…" Shake was just about over all the polite palaver and Buddhist grace from a gang of kidnapers. "Mr. Ngo sent me here as his representative. And one of my tasks is to ensure Mrs. Ngo and her sister are well and confirm that with Mr. Ngo. That's part of my deal, and I intend to live up to it. You guys want to sit in on the call, I don't give a shit. But I'm making that call."

Big Boss bristled as much as his stoic countenance allowed. He stared hard and Shake stared right back. Finally, Big Boss spun on the heels of his plastic sandals and motioned for Shake to follow him back to the little command post. He retrieved the sat phone and handed it over, standing well within reach as Shake mashed a preset to make the call.

"Walt? Checking in here to let you know I've talked to Chesa and her sister."

"They OK? Anything wrong on your end?"

"Not so far. They tell me we're leaving for Myawaddy in the morning. No idea when we'll arrive but if the trip out is any measure, probably late tomorrow or the day after. If they let me, I'll send sitreps along the way."

"OK, Shake. Good. Listen, if there's anything you can do to push them along, do it."

"Might put us up at the exchange point after dark…"

"Better that way, Shake. You know, sleepy border guards, fewer patrols, things like that."

Shake ended the call and handed the sat phone back to Big Boss. Better in the dark? Didn't sound right. Didn't sound completely wrong either. And Walt Ngo seemed confident enough. Likely just antsy to get his wife back in one piece. Yet he couldn't get rid of an uneasy tingle in his gut.

In one of the little bedrooms off the main corridor, Shake and Pete were served a bland meal of rice and shrimp. Not much but not bad. And green tea was welcome. Pete got the serving woman to bring another pot and a plastic jug of water that they could drink if they got thirsty during the night.

He stood looking out a second-story window, watching inky shadows rise as the sun fell. Someone had driven Pete's old Defender inside the walls and there were two guards milling around it. He was worried they intended to detail search the vehicle. His rucksack, passport, and cash were in there plus the two guns tucked away under a floorboard. The goons never even looked. They were interested in the jerry-cans strapped to the fenders.

"You're about to lose some fuel, Pete." The guards pulled one of the cans loose and carried it toward a battered road-weary truck parked nearby. The butt-ugly vehicle was probably ex-military, slightly smaller and squattier than an old GI deuce-and-a-half. A pitted logo on the tailgate said it was a Dongfeng A gift of the Chinese via Hanoi and Vientiane likely. The new owners had painted over the OD with a color that hit the spectrum somewhere between pea soup and puke.

"Sunnabeech…" Pete joined him at the window and shook his head. One of the guards pulled a greasy rag out of the fueling access pipe while his buddy hoisted Pete's jerry-can and sloshed diesel into the truck's tank. "Cost very much this gas…"

"We gonna have enough to make it back to Myawaddy?"

"Maybe. If no…maybe can buy little bit on road. You can pay, Shek?"

"I think Mr. Ngo will spring for a tank of diesel, Pete."

There were no lights in their little room and when Pete tried to get out to the hallway to ask about that, they found the door securely locked. There was just one rickety rattan chair between the sleeping mats. Pete slumped in it and poured tea while Shake reclined and tried to stretch some of the tension out of his body. The tingle had moved from his gut to his spine, but he still couldn't spot the cause. There was just something a little bit off, a little bit flaky…

"Wonder how the KNP found out they were holding the wife of a very rich man…"

"Guard tell me they get call…" Pete shrugged and slurped tea. "He say somebody Yangon tell everyone be on lookout for Missus Chesa."

Uh-huh. And the jungle drums start thumping. Shake put his hands behind his head and stared at the ceiling. Walt Ngo, the very rich man in question, raises hell with the government in Rangoon about his missing wife. The politicians put the word out to the Tatmadaw. Tatmadaw alerts the countryside militia, and one of those local weasels tells the KNP—which just happens to have a goon squad out in the bush holding a couple of females headed for resale.

"Missus Chesa have very strong Nat." Pete stretched out on the opposite sleeping mat. "Guard say one-eye man want to fook Missus Chesa…then cut off head. Miss Endra he sell."

"Buddha and The Nats." Shake chuckled. Buddha and The Nats singing do-wop tunes out in the jungle hoping for a hit. The tingle eased a bit.

"Big Boss…"

"Name Pha Pat. Other one glasses name Miyat Win."

"Whatever. Big Boss said we were taking back roads on the way back to Myawaddy. Why do that?"

"Maybe so not run into Tatmadaw…"

"You'd think these guys would have the local Tatmadaw on their payroll."

"Maybe so in Moulmein. Other places, different Tatmadaw."

"And all of them have got their hands out for money."

"Is Burma, Shek…" Pete yawned and rolled over. In moments he was snoring softly.

Shake continued to stare into the darkness. *Ship me somewhere east of Suez, where the best is like the worst, where there aren't no Ten Commandments an' a man can raise a thirst…*

၏

Soft sunlight was just creeping in through the window when the door to their room clicked open. Cyclops was standing there with his rifle pointed at them. He had an extra knapsack strapped on his waist near a machete and an old metal GI canteen. He stepped back and pointed at the hallway. Road trip.

"Heave out and trice up, Pete. Looks like we're getting an early start." Shake nudged Pete awake and then splashed some water into his hand and doused his face.

Out in the courtyard, the KNP truck was idling roughly with four goons standing around it. Big Boss walked out of the building suited up for a safari into the Kalahari. He had a pith helmet mashed onto his bald head and several devices including Shake's sat phone peeking from the pockets of a bush jacket straight out of Panama Jack. No luggage or pack. There were enough zippers, snaps, and pockets on his outfit to hold anything he could possibly need for the trip.

Big Boss nodded at Shake and then held a lengthy conversation with Pete. Lots of finger shaking and arm waving. When it was over, Pete crawled into the Defender and cranked the engine. "He say Missus Chesa and Miss Endra go in truck. We follow truck."

Chesa Ngo and her sister Endra appeared, arm in arm heading for the back of the truck. They had been given an admixture of bush ensembles, which looked newly purchased, probably by one of the female guards over in Moulmein. Chesa was dressed in explorer chic including sturdy boots and cargo pants. Her sister wore an oversized khaki shirt over one of the typical Burmese female tube skirts. Chesa waved at Shake and Pete in the idling Defender and ignored the hand Big Boss offered as she pulled Endra into the back of the truck.

Big Boss chained the tailgate and climbed into the cab of the truck beside the driver. Four goons in back, driver and Big Boss in front. Enemy order of battle six, maybe seven if Cyclops showed up. And nine rounds for the .45 under his feet plus a bag of buckshot shells for Pete's scattergun. Might be OK should the sewage strike the propellors.

"Where's Little Boss?"

"Miyat Win stay here." Pete clutched and grabbed a gear as the truck began to roll toward the gate. "Phone call alla time from Pha Pat."

Shake was about to ask about Cyclops when the man appeared carrying two plastic water jugs. He heaved them into the back seat and crawled in after them. He shifted around a bit and then laid the muzzle of his ratty old M-16 on the top of the front bench seat with the muzzle pointed at Shake. The rifle had some mileage, plastic handguard cracked and taped in a few places, but it looked like it would still work when required.

Pete slowly steered into trail behind the truck keeping enough distance to avoid choking plumes of diesel exhaust. It didn't do much for the atmosphere inside the Defender. Cyclops pulled a pack of Chinese Double Happiness smokes from a pocket and lit up. He didn't offer to share but he did toss Shake's GPS into the front seat and grunted something at Pete.

"Pak say when we come Myawaddy, you use machine to find gold place."

"Roger…copy all." Shake fiddled with the GPS. About half power but after a little searching, the machine found itself and showed an icon just shy of Burma highway AH-1. Road distance to Myawaddy 120 K. He keyed a waypoint and hit transmit. Unless Big Boss decided to let him use the sat phone, he couldn't talk to Walt Ngo and Chris Anthony, but they could follow the GPS signal as long as the batteries lasted.

Not much to say anyway. They were on the road with Chesa and Endra in the truck just ahead and inbound Myawaddy. Everything according to plan. If the gold was where it was supposed to be, if the KNP played it straight, he'd get the women across the river into Thailand and Mike Charlie…Mission Complete.

Shake shook down his can of Copenhagen and stuffed a pinch into his lower lip. The buzz competed with that nagging tingle and he tried to relax.

ၚၑ

The term back roads vastly understated the case. For the past five hours they'd crawled along behind the KNP truck, watching it sway nearly to the point of overturning as the driver rolled it over huge roots and rocks. Pete rarely got beyond third gear which gave him plenty of opportunity to roll redolent smokes. Cyclops in the backseat added to the miasma burning through a pack of Double Happiness.

The only break came when the convoy stopped to let everyone stretch and pee. Shake gratefully ducked out of the smoke cloud and escorted Chesa and Endra into the bushes. He glared at the gawkers who tried to sneak a peek. They glared back but didn't seem anxious to make an issue of it.

Chesa Ngo took a seat next to him during one of the breaks and he passed her a bottle of water. She swallowed about half of it and fanned her hands in front of her face.

"You doing OK, Chesa?"

"Exhaust fumes…" She spit a mouthful of water on the ground. "And the men riding with us could all use a shower."

"You've got nothing on me. Between Pete and that one-eyed goon, I'll probably come down with terminal lung cancer."

"How long until Myawaddy?"

Shake looked up through the trees that formed a canopy over the road and checked his watch. "We're not making any time on this goat path. I guess, it depends on whether they decide to stop somewhere for the night. If so, we'll probably make the border before noon tomorrow."

"I wish they would just press on. I want this nightmare to be over." She looked at her sister who was standing near the truck chatting with Big Boss. "I need to get my sister away from these people."

"She giving you problems?"

"So naïve…" Chesa shook her head and sipped water. "She's never been anywhere but our little village. And these men are filling her head with nationalist nonsense. I think they're trying to talk her into staying with them."

"Can't imagine that would be a good thing."

"No…it wouldn't. They talk about fighting for freedom, about an independent Karen nation, about overthrowing the government in Yangon."

"Yeah, wild-eyed radicals with their hair on fire. Fight to the death against their oppressors. I've seen it before. Never ends well when the oppressors have more money, guns, and lawyers." The truck's engine fired, and Big Boss shouted for everyone to reboard.

"Endra thinks she would become some kind of heroine." Chesa stood and finished off the water. "She'd wind up scrubbing floors and sleeping with whichever animal wanted her."

"Well, I told your husband I'd get both of you back across the border." Shake walked to the truck and helped her up into the back. "And that's what I intend to do. Don't worry. If I have to hogtie Endra, I know how to do that."

The GPS put them a little over halfway to Myawaddy when the convoy halted. Shake stood on a running board and saw a ratty little man with what looked like an Uzi or similar bullpup subgun hanging from his shoulder. He was involved in an intense conversation with the truck driver who was waving at a large tree trunk that had been dragged across the road. Big Boss dismounted and the conversation got heated.

The Uzi man backed off a step or two and leveled his weapon.

At a signal from Big Boss, a couple of guards bailed out of the truck and stormed into the shouting match. Cyclops kicked open the rear door on his side of the Defender and strode toward the scene as he jacked a round into the chamber of his M-16.

"Looks like it's getting serious, Pete." Shake was prying at the floorboard beneath his feet and worrying about a cross-fire that might send rounds through the truck canvas at Chesa and Endra. With the goon gone, he had a chance to retrieve his pistol. He nodded at Pete. "Go on up there and see what's happening. I'm gonna get my pistol, but leave your shotgun hidden. We don't want them to know we've got weapons."

Pete nodded and trotted up the trail. Shake found the 1911, chambered a round and flicked up the safety. Hopefully that mechanism on the old pistol still worked. He jammed it into his waistband and sat back to watch.

If the little dude with the Uzi thought his weapon and an old, uprooted tree were going to stop Big Boss and the goon squad, he was sorely mistaken. He was also sorely ass-kicked when Cyclops came abreast of the fray. He didn't hesitate to stroke the highwayman in the ear with the butt of his M-16. As his victim reeled backward, Cyclops snatched the Uzi off his shoulder and ripped a machete from his belt. The guy wisely beat retreat with Cyclops whacking him on the ass with the flat part of his own machete. Shouts and laughter chased the man into the jungle as the goons shoved the roadblock out of the way.

Pete came trotting back to the Defender looking worried. "That man…" he waved vaguely at the jungle. "He want Pha Pat pay money for use road. Pha Pat tell him no…"

"And Cyclops kicked his ass. I saw that. Who was he?"

"I think maybe drug run man. Lots of drug man use road like this one."

If the little guy was part of a drug smuggling outfit, why was he the only one manning the roadblock? Hyenas run in packs. Where were his buddies? And why would drug runners who usually try to stay ultra-low profile try to shake down an outfit like the KNP?

Pete climbed back behind the wheel as Cyclops trotted back to reclaim his seat. "I think maybe have trouble now."

"Why, Pete? Looked to me like that guy got his ass kicked."

Pete shook his head and looked worried. "Drug man beat up, look weak like baby. Very angry." He waved a hand at the dense jungle on either side of the road. "Maybe many more drug man out there."

About an hour later as the convoy negotiated a sharp bend in the track, "many more drug man" showed up and opened fire. They had some weapons that fired full-auto and an early burst ripped into the left front tire of the lead truck. Shake saw rents in the truck's canvas and followed Cyclops on the run up the road toward muzzle flashes deeper into the jungle.

Cyclops took cover near the front of the disabled truck and started cranking M-16 rounds at the muzzle flashes. It looked like there were at least a half-dozen shooters. Four on the left and two on the right. One of the guards bailing out of the truck took a round and did a header into the dirt. Not dead but down hard. Shake grabbed the man's M-16 as three other guards bailed to get into the fight. The pistol in his waistband wouldn't do much good in this situation and he wanted to preserve that weapon for later as needed.

Chesa and Endra were wisely lying prone behind a jumble of water cans and boxes. As he struggled with the chain to drop the tailgate, a round blew through the canvas and penetrated a water jug which soaked the women. It also made it easier for Shake to slide them out of the truck. He hung the rifle around his neck and grabbed Chesa's arm with one hand and got hold of Endra's ankle with the other. He heaved and they slid out of the truck landing in a pile on top of him.

The full-auto fire was coming from the left, so he pulled the women to the right and into the jungle. Not much cover but the dense foliage would provide some concealment. "Keep your head down…stay low." He pressed the women down into a lush growth of elephant ears and paused to assess the fight.

Lots of rounds were flying as Cyclops and the goons blazed away at muzzle flashes. If they were doing any damage to the opposing shooters, it wasn't obvious. Except for the single guard hit in the opening fusillade, the goons seemed to be holding their own, bobbing up and down to fire from cover behind the truck. Easy to see the shooters positions against the dark green of the jungle but they were doubtless firing from cover of some kind.

The goons didn't look like they were up for charging out of the beaten zone to establish fire superiority. Standoff. Just swapping bullets. Either stay hunkered down until one side or the other ran out of ammo or start picking these guys off one by one. Shake checked the M-16. Round in the chamber and what looked like a full load in the twenty-round mag. No time for a field strip. He'd have to hope the old rifle worked as advertised. He flicked the selector to semi and moved cautiously deeper into the bush. Shake had flashes of at least a hundred jungle ambushes he'd survived in Vietnam. Déjà vu all over again.

He heard a rustle and mumbled conversation near a stand of hardwood and moved toward the sound. A shooter in ratty shorts and t-shirt was struggling with the action of an old Moson-Nagant bolt gun. The rifle had a hung round in the chamber and the shooter was cursing, struggling to extract it. Shake shouldered the M-16 and put two rounds in the man's back. Rifle worked as advertised. And thank you, Eugene Stoner.

The shooter's buddy suddenly popped up from the bush nearby looking startled with his own rifle hanging across his belly. He was raising an M-16 when Shake put another pair center mass in the man's chest. He retrieved the dead man's rifle plus a couple of the loaded M-16 magazines and retreated, looking for a safe place to cross the road and deal with the shooters on the other side.

Cyclops and the goons didn't appear to be doing much other than popping useless rounds into the bush. There was a steady stream of incoming that kept them ducking and dodging. Shake saw Big Boss squatted behind a front tire jabbering into the cell phone pressed to his ear. Maybe there was a KNP bush unit nearby. More likely there was a Tatmadaw patrol that would be coming to investigate the firefight before too long. They had to get out of this shit-sandwich and roll for Myawaddy.

Shake maneuvered along the right side of the road until he came to the Defender stopped about thirty meters behind the truck. Pete was on his belly underneath the vehicle. He was smart enough not to reveal his shotgun just yet and it wouldn't add much advantage to the fight anyway. Shake tossed him the spare M-16 and pointed at the bush on the left side of the road.

"Cover! And tell the goons up there to cease fire…" The old soldier knew exactly what Shake had in mind. He shouted some commands in Burmese and the firing from the truck petered out as Pete started popping rounds at an angle up the road. Shake darted across and began to feel for the flank of the ambush force.

He found it after just a few steps and caught one of the men cycling rounds through what looked like an old British SMLE rifle. He never saw Shake behind him. Two rounds dropped him decisively and Shake switched magazines before moving on toward the full-auto shooter. It sounded like the man was firing from somewhere ahead and to Shake's right. The weapon had an odd popping sound that he couldn't identify as the gunner fired short, controlled bursts. This guy was no amateur.

When Shake finally spotted him, he was startled to see the gunner and an assistant crouched behind an ancient Japanese Type 96 Light Machine Gun. The assistant was snapping another curved 30-round mag into place atop the gun when Shake walked three rounds into his shoulder and up into his neck. The gunner struggled wildly to pivot the gun on its bipod. He gave up when Shake aimed and put a round into the receiver of the old Nambu. The gunner spun and tore through the dense bush thrashing and shouting. Shake spotted another man scrambling to retreat and decided not to fire or pursue. It was over.

He spent a moment examining the old Nambu. *Where the hell did they get that?* Leftover from World War II. Had to be. And apparently there were still some 6.5mm Arisaka rounds for it. The damn thing should be in a museum somewhere. He stood pondering when Big Boss showed up to examine the carnage.

"It would seem you have some military experience, Mr. Davis." He pointed at the dead a-gunner and nodded toward the other side of the road. "I saw the bodies."

"Yeah…" Shake tossed him the M-16 and shrugged. "Been there, done that a time or two."

Shake walked back to the road where surviving goons were gathered around the truck. The hood was raised and one of them was poking around the engine compartment. Pete arrived and caught a lethal glare from Cyclops who spun on a heel and stomped off into the bush at the roadside. Chesa was doing her best to bandage the wounded man and it looked like he'd survive. Endra was standing nearby trembling, eyes wide, taking in the carnage along the road. She was about to see some more.

Cyclops dragged one of the corpses onto the road near the truck. His fellow goons shied away as he drew his machete and began to hack at the dead man's neck. Shake was on the other side of the truck when it started. He heard a sound like a butcher chopping meat with a clever and ducked around to see Cyclops complete the cut through muscle, tendon and vertebrae to completely behead his victim.

Shake had to fight the urge to pull the pistol from his waistband and shoot Cyclops dead right there. The sick sonofabitch deserved it. Cyclops lifted the severed head and tossed it into the bush. He was heading for victim two when Big Boss arrived and began to scream at him. After a few minutes of berating, Cyclops shrugged, wiped the machete clean on the dead man's shirt and hung it back on his waist.

Endra had witnessed it all. She was on her knees retching in giant heaves. Chesa ran to her side with a bottle of water and an evil glare at Cyclops. Big Boss was mightily pissed off, sputtering, speechless. He stood glaring with hands on his hips as Cyclops sauntered away to light a cigarette. Shake walked up beside him, pointed at the headless corpse, and raised his eyebrows. "What the hell was that?"

"This is not typical of the Karen National Progressive Party, Mr. Davis! We fight for the people of Myanmar. We do not condone such actions!"

"Yeah, well…" Shake pointed at Cyclops. "One of your men condones it. You need to get a grip on that guy."

"It will be handled, I assure you. Pak will be disciplined!"

"Let me know how that goes." Shake walked away from the scene shaking his head. "If it doesn't work, I'll gladly shoot the evil bastard for you."

He stopped by Chesa who was hugging her sobbing sister and knelt to see if he could help. "Ugly stuff, Chesa." He put a soothing hand on Endra's heaving back. "She shouldn't have to see something like that." Chesa nodded and whispered. "If nothing else, I think it changed her mind about the KNP."

Shake nodded and rose to check on damage to the truck. It was getting late, and they needed to get on the road. Back behind the cab it didn't look too bad. Lots of bullet holes in the frame and canvas. One tire shredded. The man who was checking the engine compartment jumped down from the front fender and offered his assessment. Apparently, it wasn't good.

Big Boss checked his watch. "I think we will be delayed getting to Myawaddy." He pulled Shake's sat phone from his jacket. "You should call Mr. Ngo and let him know we have run into some difficulties. He should expect us tomorrow."

Shake really didn't want to do that. He was still worried about the Tatmadaw or some other local authority showing up to investigate the firefight. "Let me take a look. Maybe we can get this thing back on the road." He walked up toward the front of the truck. Where is Triple A when you need them? But Pete was a pretty fair shade-tree mechanic, and he was already up to his elbows in the engine compartment. "I'm guessing we can fix the tire." Shake had spotted a couple of spares in the back of the truck. "What's the engine look like?"

Pete jumped down from the front fender holding a length of V-shaped rubber. Fan belt. And Auto Zone or Pep Boys probably didn't have a parts outlet anywhere nearby. "Bullet cut belt." Pete didn't seem overly worried. "Water pump OK."

"Damn, Pete. I really wanted to get to Myawaddy today."

"Is OK, Shek. I maybe can fix."

Big Boss was dubious but happy with the possibility that he might not have to delay the exchange. He let Pete get to work in an attempt to manufacture a new fanbelt for the truck.

It was a marvel of ingenuity. Pete took Shake's sturdy old leather belt and another about the same width and composition from one of the goons. He cut the buckles off then measured, trimmed, and shaped using a razor-sharp machete. When the jury-rig belt was right, he nailed it together with a pair of rivets he found in his tool kit and then wrapped the connection in about a mile of duct tape. Shake manned a socket wrench and helped him adjust the tension. It looked horrible but spun nicely when the driver fired up the engine. After that, the tire repair was a snap. Improvise, adapt and overcome. The Marine Corps would be proud of Pete.

They were on the road less than two hours after the first shot was fired in the ambush. Shake punched another waypoint into the GPS. If the fanbelt held and they continued to roll on uninterrupted, he figured to make Myawaddy by midnight.

ဂဏ

Lieutenant Ma Puyet squatted in the clearing examining some of the expended brass. Little wonder his reconnaissance platoon was sent to investigate. This was a major firefight. Likely between two drug smuggling outfits. Three dead and one of those beheaded. A turf battle surely. He glanced over at the two prisoners his men had strapped to a nearby bullet-riddled tree. Those two smugglers were on the losing side, and they claimed the winners were from the Karen National Progressive Party. And there was a white man with them? Nonsense. The Recon Platoon commander knew this part of his AO. It was shot through with drug runners who fought like rabid dogs for territory this close to the border. And any white men involved were on the other side of the border in Thailand.

Lt. Ma Puyet called for his radioman and waited for the man to affix the long antenna which would put him in touch with his commanding officer at Light Infantry Battalion 275. A fight like this one so close to Myawaddy would be of interest. Colonel Moan was determined to clear his district of smugglers. At least those who did not pay for safe passage.

ဂဏ

Lieutenant Colonel Na Moan stood in his command post just outside the Myawaddy airstrip and listened to the report from his Recon Platoon. He trusted his man who had plenty of experience dealing with the bands of rebels, smugglers and drug runners that permeated his area of operations. Lt. Ma Puyet was likely correct in his assessment of the clash out in the jungle. It happened all the time.

Colonel Na Moan tried to maintain a delicate balance in such matters. Many of the groups smuggling drugs or females paid handsomely to avoid his patrols. The occasional smuggling band that stumbled into one of his units in the jungle provided just enough activity to convince Yangon that he was in full and effective control of this region so close to the Thai border.

He pressed the transmit switch on his radio. "You have prisoners?"

"Two of them…" Lt. Ma Puyet replied. "And some of the weapons they were using in the fight."

Two prisoners and some weapons. It would make a good show for his report to Yangon. "I'm sending the helicopter. Bring them in for interrogation. And bring the weapons."

Lieutenant Colonel Na Moan tossed the radio handset to his duty officer with instructions to send the unit's only helicopter out to retrieve the Recon Platoon and their prisoners. What concerned him as he walked back to his office were indications that the survivors of the clash were headed east toward Myawaddy, toward the border. And a white man involved somehow? He needed further information.

Likely it would turn out to be routine, but Colonel Na Moan was a cautious man. And he had an old soldier's instincts. The business about the KNP and the white man was curious. It could be nonsense. Or it could be the damned KNP stirring the pot. They had spies and activists all over, little bands of troublemakers who preached anarchy and recruited malcontents from the villages throughout Kayin State. And anything to do with the Karen National Progressive Party was of singular interest to Yangon. They were at the very top of Tatmadaw's list of banned Ethnic Armed Organizations.

In his office, the CO of Light Infantry Battalion 275 sat staring at a map of his area. It was puzzling. What would the KNP be doing so close to the border? And with a white man in tow, if there was any truth to the initial report. Suppose the KNP had cooked up some kind of deal to obtain weapons in Thailand. Suppose the white man was an arms dealer? They could bring weapons and explosives across the river at any of several fording points where the Thaung Yin ran narrow and shallow. And the damn Friendship Bridges between Mae Sot and Myawaddy were a joke. Most of the Border Guards were former rebels. The greedy bastards would ignore a howitzer if enough money changed hands.

On his way to an evening meal in the officers' mess, Lieutenant Colonel Na Moan stopped by the command post and pointed at the duty officer. "Patrols tonight. Squads to sweep the river north and south of the bridges." Probably overkill, but if the KNP is up to something, he'd rather be safe than sorry.

၇၀၃

Pete leaned on the Defender's horn signaling the truck ahead of them to stop. They were running dangerously short of fuel. Pete said he knew of a place where they could get diesel, but it meant they'd have to leave the back roads and steer onto the AH-1 highway.

"Is there a problem?" Big Boss climbed out of the truck and walked to meet Shake.

"We need fuel. My driver says he knows where we can get some." Shake showed the GPS where an icon blinked near a little village on the north side of the main highway. "I can pay to fill up our vehicle and yours. That way you won't have to stop again on your way back with the gold."

Big Boss studied the GPS. "It would mean traveling on the main roads." He chewed on his lower lip for a moment. "Perhaps we could buy fuel at this place and then get back on the smaller roads. Camp for the night and go to Myawaddy in the morning."

"Bad idea..." Shake pointed up at the darkening sky. "Mr. Ngo has had your gold sitting out there for a while now. He's probably got somebody guarding it, but what if the Army, the cops or somebody sees it and starts asking questions. We don't want that, right? If we stay on the highway, push for Myawaddy and get this deal done, you'll be on the road back to Moulmein with the gold by dawn."

"There may be Army patrols or checkpoints."

Shake pulled the official clearance letter from the State Ministry of Religious Affairs and Culture out of his pocket and handed it over. "This is our pass." He waited while Big Boss studied the letter. "We run into the Tatmadaw and that letter gets us a free pass. I've used it before with no problems. All you guys have to do is keep your weapons hidden and your mouth shut. I'll do the rest."

Either Big Boss was greatly impressed by the official document from Rangoon, or he was reluctant to spend a night in the jungle if he didn't have to. He nodded agreement and had Pete lead the convoy onto a little access road that intersected with AH-1.

၇၃၂

They turned eastward and about a half-hour later Pete coasted the Defender on fumes into a little village. It was just another wide spot in the road, but a generator was humming somewhere in the surrounding jungle. The lights were on, and people were milling around a little tea and sandwich shack near a larger structure festooned with derelict cars, spare tires and an admixture of auto parts. Shake didn't see any kind of gas pump, but Pete immediately headed for a stack of plastic jugs under a standing light at the side of the bigger building. A stocky guy in greasy shorts and a tank top walked out of the shop wiping his hands and nodded at Pete.

The proprietor looked around wide-eyed, taking in the beat-up old Defender and the puke green truck parked nearby. Both vehicles looked like they'd been involved in some serious combat, which was clearly not something he saw regularly in the middle of the night at his little roadside facility.

Shake noticed the man eyeing the bullet-scarred vehicles as he helped Chesa and Endra down from the truck. Did the guy have a phone? And if he did, was he likely to use it to report a couple of obviously battle-damaged vehicles dropping by his little shop to refuel?

While Pete chatted with the proprietor, Shake led Chesa and Endra toward the tea shop where they dickered with an older woman behind a small counter. Endra seemed to be feeling better. Revulsion at what she'd seen on the road had passed for now. She was stoic and stuck to her sister like glue. Shake called that a good sign as he passed Chesa some money to pay for their orders. Chesa got some extra for the wounded goon and walked away as Big Boss ducked under the canvas to report he'd given orders to his men for the remainder of the trip.

Cyclops and the goons dismounted stretching and complaining. All their weapons except for a few standard machetes or bush knives hanging from their belts were hidden underneath tarps in the truck bed. They didn't like not being strapped with firepower, but they were cooperating.

Shake pulled up his left sleeve and pointed at his watch. "Figure twenty minutes to refuel and get something to eat. We should be at the exchange point around midnight." He pointed at the sat phone in Pha Pat's pocket. "Better let me call Mr. Ngo and let him know."

Chris Anthony picked up on the first ring. "We show you stopped on AH-1. Everything OK?"

"Had to refuel. We'll be rolling shortly. Figure to make the exchange point around midnight. You got the stuff in place?"

"It's there. On a pallet covered with a tarp. We've got some men guarding it, but they'll disappear as soon as they see you. Have your driver flash his lights as you approach."

"Copy. And then I bring Chesa and Endra across the bridge. You guys still at the same place?"

"Irrawaddy Resort. We'll be waiting."

Shake ended the call and nodded at Big Boss. "They're all set to make the exchange. Your gold is ready for pick-up. You get that and I'm on the way to Thailand with Mrs. Ngo and her sister." Big Boss smiled and didn't object when Shake pocketed the cell phone.

Pete called and waved for Shake to join him near a pile of old tires. He was fretting. "Cost very much this gas."

"Not the time to bitch about prices, Pete." Shake reached into his pocket for the cash envelope. There was more than a grand left in green and he didn't mind spending whatever it took to get them rolling. "How much do you need?"

Pete eyed the cash and ran the tab in his head. "For two truck maybe need four…maybe six…" He waved a hand at the pile of fuel jugs. Can do eighty Yew Ess dollah, Shek?"

"Can do easy…" Shake peeled four twenties and handed them over. He eyed the mechanic who was probing one of the bullet holes in the side of the green truck and caught

Pete's elbow. "Give that guy this…" He pulled out two more twenties. "And tell him to keep his mouth shut about us."

"Is OK, Shek." Pete chuckled and waved off the extra cash. "This man say alla time Tatmadaw come take gas…never pay. He don't like Army. No worries."

ၻ၀ၬ

Lieutenant Colonel Na Moan sat in his office fretting and squirming. He'd spent the past two hours interrogating the two drug smugglers captured by his Recon unit. Despite several sound beatings, both men stuck to their story. They insisted that they'd been in a gunfight with men from the KNP. One of them told a story about stopping two trucks and being beaten by a one-eyed man who identified himself as KNP. Said they were from Moulmein in Mon State.

If that was so, what were they doing here? They must be heading for Myawaddy or somewhere close by. There were KNP sympathizers in his area. Col. Moan knew about them, but they'd always maintained a low profile. It just didn't sit well with him, and he was feeling some heartburn that was not caused by the crappy dinner he'd just eaten.

He'd been badly treated after a major fight with Karen and Mon tribal factions up near the Three Pagodas Pass. That encounter lasted nearly a week and cost him in both manpower and reputation at Tatmadaw headquarters in Yangon. And now the damn rebels might be gearing up for another offensive along his stretch of the border. That he would not tolerate. He had patrols out along the river but that might not be enough. The KNP was a worry, a treacherous and stealthy lot that just might be colluding with compatriots or supporters in Thailand. Why chance that?

He reached for his phone and tapped in the number for the duty officer at the Border Guard Police headquarters in Myawaddy. "Col. Moan here. I want to speak to your commander immediately." He lit a cigarette and blew smoke into the humid air as he waited for the commander of the Border Guard Police at Myawaddy town. The man was a greedy idiot, but he feared the power of the Tatmadaw.

It took nearly ten minutes for the duty officer to find his commanding officer and get him to the phone. Col. Moan wasted no time when he heard the sleepy voice on the other end of the line.

"Close the bridges immediately."

The Border Guard Police CO was wide awake now and complaining about the problems involved with shutting down traffic across Friendship Bridges. The flow of traffic across the river to and from Thailand went on all night every night. It was the lifeblood of commerce on both sides of the river.

"I am aware of the problems." Col. Na Moan growled into the phone. "And I am also the senior Tatmadaw officer. Now close the bridges and keep them closed until further notice."

၏

They hit a final Army checkpoint on AH-1 just five kilometers from the designated exchange point. The sky was pitch black when Pete stopped the Defender near a barrier of orange traffic cones. Only three men on duty and two of them were asleep in a couple of chairs outside a slapdash little guard shack. Wearing his camera around his neck, Shake dismounted with the authorization letter and handed it to Pete.

When Pete finished a long-winded conversation with the soldier on duty, he handed over the letter and both men moved into the cone of the Defender's headlights. The soldier squinted at the letter for a while as Pete stood nearby waving his hands and pointing at Shake who just stood smiling and fiddling with the camera.

Something was wrong. This was taking too long. Shake eyed the truck idling behind the Defender and saw Cyclops' single eye glaring over the top of the cab. Shake gave him a thumbs up hoping the lunatic didn't start shooting as Pete stepped up beside him and whispered. "Soldier no can read. Don't understand paper."

Shake thought about just running the roadblock and then had a better idea. He opened the back hatch and rummaged around in his rucksack. If it worked once, it might work twice. He pulled a copy of *Mortal Combat*, wrapped it in a twenty-dollar bill and handed it to Pete. "Try this."

The illiterate soldier pocketed the cash and examined the videogame in the glow of the headlights. Wearing a big grin, he woke one of his buddies to help him move the traffic cones. They were rolling two minutes later.

ෙ෴

Following the GPS directions, they made good time. It was just 15 minutes after one in the morning when Shake directed Pete to make a final left turn off the road and flash his headlights. There was no response, but Shake could see a tarp in the center of the clearing covering a pyramid shape atop a wooden pallet. The area seemed to be deserted. Anthony said there were guards, but Shake couldn't see anyone. Probably melted back into the surrounding bush as ordered when they saw the headlight signal.

He dismounted telling Pete to swing the Defender around pointed at the road to Myawaddy and keep it idling. He wanted to get this done and get the women across the river. Big Boss and Cyclops approached shining flashlights on the tarp covered pile in the middle of the clearing.

Shake snapped on his own trusty little Surefire mag-lite and swept the beam around the clearing. Still no one in sight, but likely there was some sort of armed guard lurking. Nobody leaves a mil or better in gold sitting in a jungle clearing without someone to scare off curious locals or potential thieves. As he approached the treasure trove, it occurred to Shake that some jungle viper might have decided to nest under that tarp, so he carefully grabbed an edge and pulled it free.

No snakes but his light glinted off 16 neatly stacked gold bars. Each one was etched just like the one he'd seen in Bangkok. How Ngo and Anthony managed to get it here and keep it undetected for a day or two was beyond him. It was also irrelevant.

"There you have it." Shake watched Big Boss and Cyclops gawking at the glow from the gold in the beam of their lights. "I count sixteen bars here. Figure sixty-five or seventy thousand per bar, you're looking at more than a million dollars in gold." Big Boss ran his hand over the top bar. He was just short of drooling. Cyclops grabbed one of the bars and hefted it. Shake saw him grin for the first time since he'd encountered the evil sonofabitch.

"You happy?" Shake snapped off his light and pocketed it. Big Boss stood and offered a hand. Shake ignored it. Big Boss didn't seem to notice the slight. He was fixated on the KNP's new-found riches. Shake spun on his heel. "Deal's done. I'm gonna get the women and head for the border."

Cyclops signaled his goons to help in loading the gold as Shake walked to the back of the truck and helped Chesa and her sister to the ground. "We're all set, ladies. Let's go to Thailand."

Chesa and Endra crawled out of the truck, blinking in the dark and staring at the activity in the clearing.

"What's happening?" Chesa watched one of the goons pass with a heavy load in his hands. She pointed at Big Boss and Cyclops near the tarp. "What are they doing?"

"Collecting the ransom." Shake was trying to hustle them along, but Chesa was stopped and immobile.

"I thought the ransom was paid. Didn't you bring it to Moulmein?"

"Your husband made a deal to pay in gold rather than cash, Chesa. That's it over there…a million bucks worth."

"Oh, my God!" Chesa covered her mouth with her hand. Where in the world did Walter get a million dollars' worth of gold? He'd spent most of his available cash in the refugee camps and was complaining that they might be in serious financial trouble.

ဂၢ

Cyclops stood holding on to the one gold bar he'd pulled off the top of the pile as his men carried the others to the truck. He was contemplating murder and larceny. What if he had his men retrieve their weapons and just kill everyone involved with this deal? He very much wanted to kill that loud-mouth, soft-headed politician Pha Pat anyway. If he just had this gold for his own…

He ran a hand over the smooth metal surface of the bar, eyes wide as the beam of his flashlight illuminated the potential riches in his hand. It also illuminated something strange on his left thumb. He focused on the light and took a closer look. His thumb was smeared with gold. How could that be? He rubbed harder on the bar. More gold smeared his fingers. And underneath the smear was some sort of dull grey metal. The bars were fake! Something painted to look like gold!

Cyclops dropped the bar and screamed a warning to Big Boss. "It's a trick! These are just lead bars painted to look like gold!"

While Big Boss and the goons stood in shock at the back of the truck, Cyclops pulled his machete and charged at Shake Davis.

ဘဘ

Shake heard the shout as he and Pete were shoving Chesa and Endra in the back seat of the Defender. He turned just in time to see Cyclops bearing down on him with a machete raised. He managed to duck the first swipe and heard the machete blade crunch into metal. He spun away but a second stroke caught him across his right shoulder. Shake felt the blade bite deep and tried to ignore the pain as he drew the .45 from his waistband. He flicked at the safety and fired a wild shot into the dark. It was clearly a miss as Cyclops just spun and charged again with his machete raised. Shake adjusted aim and tried another shot but the old pistol wouldn't cooperate. He ran a hand along the top of the slide and felt a stovepipe. The cartridge case from his first round had failed to eject. He rolled on the ground trying to avoid Cyclops and clear the stoppage when he heard Endra scream. He was focused on Cyclops but in his peripheral vision he saw her pointing at something in the dark.

A staggered line of camo-clad men emerged hustling out of the tree line to the north of the clearing with their weapons at high ready. Suddenly Cyclops lost interest in killing Shake. He shouted something and sprinted toward the truck where his weapons were stored. One of the goons beat him to it and pumped a burst from his M-16 at the charging soldiers. Like trained troops, they went to ground and returned fire. The canvas cover over the truck bed began to flap wildly as rounds tore through it. Shake caught a glimpse of Big Boss sprinting away toward the bush south of the clearing.

Suddenly the night lit up with muzzle flashes and tracers crisscrossing from three directions. Pete threw himself across Chesa and her sister to protect them from incoming. Shake ducked around the other side of the vehicle and tried to get a read on what was happening in the clearing. In the glow of the truck's headlights, he IDed three shooters firing from a tree line to the west of the clearing. Maybe the hired guards? And there was crossfire from the soldiers to the north. Cyclops and a couple of the surviving KNP goons were prone under the truck and pumping rounds in the other direction.

Shake had no idea what was happening, and it didn't seem healthy to stand around investigating. Ignoring the blood that was drenching his right arm, he plowed into the front seat of the Defender and shouted for Pete to get behind the wheel.

Pete didn't need prompting. He ducked into the driver's seat, popped the clutch, and steered for Myawaddy. Shake reached over the seat with his good arm and shoved the two women down toward the floorboards. Pete kept the hammer down as bullets punched more holes in his rear quarter panel. They were rolling in high gear with the shoot-out still raging behind before Shake had the energy to ask if anyone knew what the hell had just happened.

"You would know wouldn't you Mister Davis?" Chesa was angry, shouting over the roar of the engine and the crackle of gunfire.

"One-eye man say gold no good. Is fake…" Pete hit a higher gear and popped the clutch.

"Good God!" Chesa screamed. "We could have been killed back there. How could you do something like that?"

"Believe me, Chesa…" Shake was trying to squeeze flaps of skin on his shoulder back together. "I had no idea about that. Far as I knew, your husband had a million bucks in gold waiting for us—real gold. That's what he told me and that's what I believed—until just a few minutes ago."

"So…he lied to you?" Chesa was calmer now, thinking it all over. "And he risked everything on a trick? A stupid bait and switch trick?"

"It damn sure looks that way, Chesa. I don't know what to tell you, except that I had nothing to do with it. Don't shoot the messenger."

"If you are telling me the truth…" Chesa hugged her sister in the back seat, craning to look back at the light show behind them. She was confused but she'd come to trust Shake Davis. She felt he was a good man. "You don't have to tell me anything but the truth. I am very grateful for what you did to get us out of there."

Shake sat silent feeling blood run down his right bicep. It looked like Walter Ngo had pulled some kind of scam with fake metal painted to look like real gold. Even if the KNP eventually discovered they'd been cheated, what could they do about it? Their hostages would be long gone. They'd have to settle for the one gold bar worth 65 thou on the market. It was a neat little slight-of-hand deal if it had worked. But it didn't.

Hard to figure. What kind of asshole risks his wife and sister-in-law in that kind of carny-show grift? Walter Ngo has some serious explaining to do…assuming I can get back across the border and find him.

Shake had no idea if they would be pursued. Given the uneven level of firepower back in the clearing, Big Boss and Cyclops would likely be shackled guests of the Tatmadaw if they survived. He wasn't worried about that. But the soldiers had to see the Defender speeding away from the scene. And soldiers had radios. As soon as the shooting stopped, and they sorted through the mess they'd be looking for the squirters who fled in a beat-up Land Rover. And then they'd put out the local version of an APB. They needed to get across a bridge into Thailand before that happened.

Shake drew several deep breaths and tried to slow his heart rate. One problem at a time. He was leaking blood from the machete cut and he didn't want to chance passing out, so he had Pete pull over where they could take a quick look at his damaged shoulder. It was aching badly, but the copious bleeding seemed to be venous rather than arterial. Cyclops and his machete had done some damage, but Shake had weathered worse wounds.

As her sister held a light, Chesa cut away Shake's blood-drenched right sleeve and examined the wound. "Deep…needs stitches."

"No time for that…" Shake tried to smile against the throbbing pain in his shoulder. "Just wrap it up and let's get moving."

Chesa opened Pete's first-aid kit and found some pads, gauze and tape. "We'll have to do with pressure to stop the bleeding for now. We can get it sutured in Mae Sot."

"Sooner we get there, the better." Shake had Pete retrieve the windbreaker from his ruck and slid it on over the bandages. He'd just have to suck it up for now. He gobbled a handful of ibuprofen tabs and chased them with water.

As Pete rolled toward Myawaddy trying to steer clear of bumps that might further damage his arm, Shake sat back and tried to figure out what happened at the ransom exchange. And what he wanted to do about what appeared to be a nearly fatal double-cross.

ၵၸ

Something out of the ordinary was happening in Myawaddy. The little town that normally hustled and bustled all night long seemed still, almost as if it was deserted. As they got nearer, rolling along the road that led to the Friendship bridges, Shake saw long lines of vehicles, all parked, most surrounded by people just milling and talking.

"That ain't right…" Shake could see several truck drivers bitching and waving their arms toward a slug of Border Guard Police with rifles slung across their chests. There was no moving traffic in either direction and it was just an hour or two before dawn when there should be a steady flow of traffic carrying merchants from the Thai side of the river. "Find a spot out of sight and then see if you can find out what's happening."

Pete wheeled the Defender into a dark alley short of the vehicle jam-up and dismounted. "What is it?" Chesa craned around to stare into the dark. "I can't see anything."

"Some kind of jam-up at the bridges. Let's just wait and see what Pete finds out." Shake checked his sat phone. Power indicated about a third of full charge. It also showed three missed calls. All from Walter Ngo and Chris

Anthony's contact number. Had to be those guys were aware that their scam had been busted and the deal gone sour. They had armed guards posted…and the guards watching over what they thought was a fortune in gold would be in radio or phone contact.

And somehow Tatmadaw was involved. No question those troopers gunning out of the tree line were Army. Were they there after the KNP or the gold? If they wanted the gold…or what they thought was gold…why not just fire up the guards and make off with it? Shake needed answers.

He considered returning the calls and burning through a few asses at the Irrawaddy Resort. And then he had second thoughts. Better to save what battery power the phone retained. And calm down a bit. He was in no shape, mood, or disposition to listen to half-ass excuses or explanations on the phone. When he got their story, he wanted it to be in person so he could decide for himself what to do about it.

Pete came back to the Defender puffing on one of his hand-rolls. "Bridges closed. People very piss off. Say Army orders. Guards stop everyone. No can cross river."

"Did they say why?"

"No man know." Pete slid behind the wheel. "Just say bridge closed. No can cross river."

Shake sat thinking. The pain from the machete slash on his shoulder was radiating across his chest. Likely some horrible corruption from the blade of Cyclops' machete was starting to travel in his bloodstream. Maybe an APB was already circulating. If the bridge closure here at Myawaddy was a result of the firefight back near the airstrip, it made sense that the Army or the cops would be looking for anyone involved, particularly anyone traveling in a bullet-riddled Land Rover Defender. He pulled the cash envelope out of his pocket and checked his bankroll. He had about eight hundred dollars and a thick wad of Burmese *kyat* remaining.

"We need a different vehicle…" He handed the cash to Pete. "Go back up there and see if you can negotiate for something that will get us to…" Shake paused and took a deep breath. He had no idea where to go even if they managed to get a new vehicle.

"Where we go?" Pete was counting the money in the envelope. "If can get new truck."

"I don't know, pal. Somewhere other than here…somewhere we can get across the border into Thailand."

"We leave my truck?" Pete sounded like he was being asked to abandon a treasured old friend to hungry wolves.

"Got to, Pete. They'll be looking for it."

As Pete wandered away into the dark, heading for the long line of vehicles stacked on the bridge road, Shake got out and went to retrieve his rucksack from the back of the Defender. It was a struggle to open the heavy rear cargo door with only one good hand. A bolt of pain drove him to his knees, and he could feel fresh blood flowing from the shoulder wound. He remembered a class in combat survival from years ago: *You can lose twenty-five percent of total blood volume in anywhere from thirty seconds to three minutes…*

As Chesa rushed to help, Shake remembered something else from that long ago class: *With significant blood loss, you'll feel weakness, disorientation, nausea. At fifty percent loss, your organs start to shut down.* He was already starting to feel the early onset of a few of those things.

Chesa was checking the wound as her sister pulled the heavy ruck and set it on the ground next to them. She said something to her sister, but Chesa just shook her head.

Shake gritted his teeth against another lightning bolt from the oozing wound "If that was an idea, I'm all ears."

"She thought we might be able to swim the river." Chesa pulled Shake's windbreaker down to start peeling off the soaked bandages. "I told her we should not try that with an open wound like this."

"And with soldiers probably patrolling all over the riverbanks." If they closed the bridges, the Tatmadaw would sure as hell be watching any local fording points.

"We need proper attention for this wound before it gets infected." Chesa was repacking the gash with fresh cotton and gauze. "I have a friend, a doctor, in a refugee camp at Three Pagodas Pass."

"Where is Three Pagodas Pass?"

"About 300 kilometers south of here."

Shake thought it over, patting his pockets and wishing fervently he hadn't lost the GPS transceiver somewhere in the firefight and escape chaos. But navigation wasn't the immediate problem. Evasion and escape were. The river crossing was out of the equation with the Army on alert and his open wound already starting to fester. Three hundred k to a crossing point and medical help. If Pete managed to get some kind of reliable vehicle that wouldn't draw attention, if they could hold a reasonable road speed and clear any checkpoints, if Chesa could keep him from bleeding out, maybe 12 or 15 hours. Long shot.

Endra had something more to say to her sister. Shake looked up at the young girl's dirt-streaked face. She seemed to be over her teenage delusions. "Another idea?"

"Not a good one…" Chesa squeezed her sister's hand and shook her head. "Endra wonders why we don't just turn ourselves into the authorities. She thinks they would escort us across the border."

"Might have worked earlier. Not now." Shake had seen way too much Burmese corruption by this time to really believe that. "We'd have a hell of a time trying to explain away all the business with the KNP." And likely we'd be tied up for weeks in legal wrangling. Or you and your sister would just wind up being held for ransom again…this time by the authorities. He almost said it aloud but decided the two women needed hope rather than more worries at this point.

"Let's wait and see how Pete does. If he can get us a good vehicle, maybe we can make it to this Three Pagodas Pass."

Mae Sot, Thailand

Busted flat. Chris Anthony's brilliant scheme was an abject failure. And it wasn't his money or his wife at risk. Walter Ngo tried to keep a lid on his temper as he glared at his fraternity brother and top-level business executive listening to the report from the Thai airborne officer who had escaped the dust-up in the clearing.

"We engaged as directed when the KNP discovered that your gold was fake." The Thai officer lit a cigarette and waved his hands. "We were not briefed on Army involvement. When they arrived, we conducted a retrograde movement and recrossed the river."

Chris Anthony spun away from the laptop where he'd been examining a scorching email from Lancer corporate headquarters in Las Vegas. "We had no idea about that, I assure you. Something went wrong obviously—and the Army was likely there to deal with the KNP."

"Who gives a shit about all that?" Walt Ngo snapped. "What happened to Chesa…to my wife?"

"I can tell you that two women and two men escaped in a Land Rover Defender. Where they went, I do not know. Last seen they were headed toward Myawaddy…on the bridge road."

"And we hear that the fucking bridges are closed…"

"Yes…" The Thai officer didn't seem at all concerned with that. "So, I would presume those in the Land Rover must be in the hands of the local authorities."

"Just one of several problems we've got right now, Walt." Chris Anthony pulled an envelope out of his briefcase and handed the balance of payment to the Thai officer. "Will you be around if we need you later?"

"We will not." The Thai officer pocketed the money. "My men and I cannot take that chance. We must return to Bangkok." He mimed a snappy little salute and left the room.

"He said four people got away." Walter Ngo began to pace. "So that would be Davis, Pete, Chesa, and her sister. Where the hell are they now? I've called the sat phone three times. No answer. We'd have heard something from our man in the Border Guard if they got nabbed trying to cross the bridges."

"You should make some calls, Walt. Local and back to Vegas when they're open for business back there."

"Fuck Vegas! I need to find Chesa and Davis."

"Better read this…" Chris Anthony spun the laptop and pointed at an open email. "The Board voted you out. It was unanimous."

Ngo slumped into a chair and scanned the email. He was slammed every way he could be. And to cover expenses for this fiasco, he'd have to liquidate his remaining Lancer stock immediately. And that was not the only way he was financially screwed. He'd also have to start selling personal assets. There were a lot of greedy hands owed money to date and likely to be a lot more before he finally got Chesa back to safety and out of this miserable shithole.

"I can't deal with this right now, Chris. I've got to find Chesa and get her across the border somehow. That's the critical thing—no matter what it costs."

"You can't do that on credit cards, Walt." Chris Anthony began to toss his things into an overnight bag. "I'm headed for Bangkok to do some damage control. I'll try to cobble together all the cash I can and get it to you."

Walter Ngo reached for the phone to check with their man in the Border Guard headquarters. Maybe Chesa and the others were detained. Maybe they just hadn't heard about it yet. If so, he would need to buy them out of custody in a hurry before more senior authorities got involved and wanted a cut of the action. He checked his watch. A few hours before he could raise his lawyers and start selling most of what he owned.

"Don't fuck it up, Chris. No more money-saving maneuvers or bright ideas. You hear me?"

༒

Pete drove up an hour after he'd left in a rattletrap Toyota minivan. Big rust patches, the windshield cracked, tires nearly bald, and the interior smelled like the previous owner had used it to transport raw sewage—but it was full of gas. And the ratty van would likely not draw any particular attention. There were hundreds of similar vehicles traversing the border roads.

They transferred Shake's ruck and some of Pete's gear from the Defender. Shake reluctantly ditched the old .45 in a garbage can near the alley where they were parked. There were only a few rounds left, and the old horse-pistol had done its job. If they needed firepower on the trip, he'd rely on Pete's scattergun. Chesa and Endra made up a little bed for him on the bench backseat. She insisted he remain prone and inactive as possible with Endra sitting on a jerry-rig rumble seat to keep him hydrated from a collection of water bottles they offloaded from the Defender. He stretched out with his head on his rucksack, covered by a poncho liner, and tried to relax. Pete climbed behind the wheel with Chesa riding shotgun next to him and they rolled south.

Traffic on the AH-1 was light and the sun was just beginning to peek over a verdant green horizon. Pete figured maybe five hours on roads that climbed steadily toward the Tenasserim Hills and the Thai Border. Shake rolled onto his side favoring the wound which was still seeping blood and tried to ignore the pain that shot through his torso with every bump in the road.

To keep himself distracted as Chesa and Pete chatted in Burmese, he searched his mind for something that had been nagging at him since first mention of Three Pagodas Pass. It wasn't the ancient, crumbling *stupas* that Chesa said were on the Thai side of the border and a popular tourist attraction. It was something else, something he'd read in a military history book.

It finally came to him when Endra cradled his head for a drink of water. It wasn't the pagodas. It was the pass through the mountains. The Japanese had pushed their infamous Death Railway through that mountain pass during World War II using POW labor. Thousands of British, American, Australian, and Dutch prisoners died in the effort. Probably make a good movie, he thought as he fell asleep, if they hadn't already done something similar in the *Bridge Over the River Kwai.*

Two hours later when he felt the minivan lean into a hard right turn, Shake woke and tried to sit up. The pain in his shoulder had faded to a deep, dull ache but when he elbowed his way up in the bench seat clotted blood peeled away from the wound. Another electric jolt of pain hit him, and he could feel blood running down his bicep.

Chesa leaned over the front seat and handed him the last of their ibuprofen tabs. "We need to change the bandages."

"That why we're stopping?"

"Eat…get gas…more water." Pete retrieved what money they had left from the car deal and waved it for Shake to see. It didn't look like much. "Still have little bit for eat and gas." When all this was over, Shake intended to see that Pete walked away with a lot more than a little bit for eat and gas.

They wheeled into what looked like a truck stop with a little restaurant nearby. Shake saw two official vehicles parked near the café. Chesa identified them as Peoples' Police Force rather than Tatmadaw. Four uniforms were milling around the vehicles drinking tea and smoking. They didn't seem overly alert or running checks on any of the trucks parked nearby.

"You stay cover up. If some man look, Miss Endra talk." Pete parked in the shade of a bamboo stand while Chesa gave Endra some instructions about what to say if the cops showed interest in their vehicle or destination. *Good plan*, Shake decided as he pulled the poncho liner over his head. He still had his legend cover letter, but that was unlikely to work if it was presented by a bloody Yank with a machete wound in his shoulder.

The sat phone vibrated and Shake checked it. Walt Ngo or Chris Anthony again, probably frantic. Good. Let the bastards stew for a while longer. Once he got the wound sewn up, dosed himself with antibiotics, and regained some strength, he'd see about getting everyone back up the road to Mae Sot for a talk with Ngo and Anthony. Until then, they could just wait and wonder. He tucked the phone away and closed his eyes.

The sound of someone banging on the outside of the vehicle woke him with a start. He tried to sit up, but Endra pushed him back down. She said something soothing and pointed at a window. Shake peeked to see Pete wrestling with the little door that provided access to the gas tank.

Chesa slid into the front seat carrying paper plates. "Gas tank lid is stuck…" She passed a plate to Endra and said something that was hard to hear over Pete's cursing. Shake reached into a pocket with his good hand and felt around for the slim little CRKT multi-tool he always carried. It was an ingenious combination knife, screwdriver, and pry-bar in a long slim design that was handier and less bulky than a Leatherman.

"Have him try this…" Shake handed over the tool and Chesa passed it along to Pete. While Pete pried and bitched outside, he watched Endra poking at a pile of fried rice with a plastic spoon. He couldn't remember the last time he'd eaten and suddenly realized he was ravenous.

"I'll have some of that, please." He made hand to mouth signs, but Endra just shook her head and pointed at her sister. "You get this." Chesa handed over a slab of mystery meat, dripping either blood or grease into a napkin. "You need the nourishment…B-12…iron." He smiled at her. She sounded so much like Chan serving a meal and describing why whatever she'd cooked was good for him.

Shake heard a squeal of rusted metal and smelled gasoline. Apparently Pete had forced access to their tank. He took the meat with his good hand and sniffed. Thin, gristly, and gamey, but he took a bite. Not filet mignon by a long stretch but not bad.

"What the hell is this?"

"Water buffalo. Full of nutrients. Eat it all and then we'll change your bandages."

When they got around to that a few minutes later, Shake didn't like the smell or the look of the deep wound. His entire shoulder was black and blue featuring some red streaks that meant it was festering. Chesa used the last of Pete's gauze and cotton, tied the bandages with an old shop towel and pulled it tight. "We need antibiotics and sutures…stat." She shifted to full nurse mode. "How are you feeling?"

"Like some asshole slashed me with a dirty machete. Other than that, pretty good."

"You've lost a lot of blood. And you're still leaking. Any nausea? Fever?"

"I'll let you know about the nausea once the water buffalo settles…" He laid back down on the seat and Chesa felt around on his forehead and neck. "Low grade fever," she said. "Be sure to drink plenty of water." She turned to Endra and gave instructions as Pete got back in the vehicle and started the engine.

"Police man say looking for Land Rover with bullet holes. Ask if I see to report." The APB was out. Not much they could do about that other than duck and dodge. Pete wheeled back onto the highway and ran through the gears. "No problem. Maybe get to Payathonsu two more hours."

"I thought we were heading for Three Pagodas Pass?"

"Payathonsu is the village on the Burma side of the Three Pagodas Pass." Chesa scrunched around in her seat. "On the other side is the Thai town of Sangklaburi and that's where we'll find my doctor friend."

"Your husband called again…" Shake was fighting to stay conscious as the hum of tires on asphalt lulled him. He felt kitten weak and fuzzy headed.

Chesa craned over her seat. "Did you talk to him?"

"No. Do you want to?"

"Not yet. I will have plenty to say to Walter, but I want to be looking into his eyes when that happens."

ဆင်း

An hour later, Pete pulled off the road again and the jolt of the brakes brought Shake out of his fog. "There's a road-block or some kind of checkpoint ahead." Chesa leaned across the seat and put a hand on Shake's forehead. "It's right where we need to turn off for the pass."

Shake elbowed himself up painfully to look through a window. Nothing but jungle surrounding a little clearing. "How do you know that?"

Chesa pointed at Pete. "He pulled off to let us all pee a little while ago. Another driver was complaining about it. Peoples' Police checking all vehicles."

Shake lay back and groaned. "And no way around it? No other road we can take?"

"There's just the one road that runs up to the pass and then across the border." She had a brief conversation with Pete and then turned back to Shake. "Pete tells me you have a letter. Something that says you are working for Walter's company?"

"Yeah…" Shake squirmed around and pulled the enve-lope containing the cover letter from his pocket. He handed it to Endra who passed it to her sister. Chesa sat reading in-tently. "Ain't gonna work though. I'm in no shape to con-vince cops I'm some kind of innocent researcher out photo-graphing the countryside."

"Maybe you won't have to." Chesa had another conver-sation with Pete in Burmese. "This letter identifies the bearer as someone researching for a videogame. It doesn't say who that bearer is…"

They buried Shake under his poncho liner in the back of the vehicle and spread an oil-stained tarp over that. Pete tucked his shotgun under the wraps and then stacked Shake's rucksack between the tarp and the back doors. If a cop wanted to take a look at the back of the vehicle, the first thing he'd see was the pack and there was not much in it that couldn't be explained reasonably.

Chesa retrieved the camera and an unworn Lancer Technologies gimme cap that Chris Anthony had provided as part of Shake's legend. He had to admit, in her safari get-up with the cap and the camera, she looked the part. More importantly, she spoke the language and knew enough about the business to run a solid bluff.

A half-hour later, Shake felt the minivan roll to a stop. He heard some conversation. Pete talking to a cop. He snaked a hand around to feel for the shotgun, hoping he wouldn't need it, and hoping it was loaded if he did. The passenger door creaked open at the front of the vehicle, and he heard Chesa launch into her pitch. She sounded bright and engaging. Charming the cops, letting them know she was just an innocent woman trying to make a living. Probably telling them she was headed for the pass for some shots of the famous three pagodas.

There was silence for a while. Probably the cops examining the letter from the Ministry of Religious and Cultural Affairs. Hopefully, these guys could read. And then he heard Chesa chattering again as the van's back doors swung open. Shake froze, trying to keep his breathing as shallow as possible. The cop was digging around in his rucksack. He found something that made him laugh. More excited chatter in Burmese. Chesa laughing and chattering like a salesman giving away free samples. It went on for a while but there was no effort to look under the tarp before the van's back doors slammed shut.

Shake felt the vehicle rock as Chesa and Pete climbed back aboard. The engine cranked and he rolled painfully as Pete swung the vehicle into a hard left and downshifted. The new road was inclining steadily upward. He peeked out from under his shrouds. "I guess we made it."

"It went well." Chesa shouted from the front seat.

"Police man see videogames!" Pete chuckled and slapped the steering wheel. "Missus Chesa give to him and he forget everything." Shake still couldn't believe the lure of a couple of stupid videogames, but he was rapidly becoming a true believer.

"The good news is we're on the road to Three Pagodas Pass…" Chesa removed the gimme cap and tossed it out her window. "Unfortunately, the policemen told me the border is closed until further notice."

ၰၥ

They climbed through a series of sharp switchbacks that slithered like a serpent up toward the pass. There was some conversation about the closed border, and the consensus seemed to be it was best to pull off the road into a scenic overlook that Pete said was just short of the border town, maybe a kilometer or a little less from Payathonsu. Shake had a pair of solid Steiner 7x50 binos in his pack that should allow a good visual reconnaissance before they decided on the next step to get across the border into Thailand.

When they finally found the overlook, it was thankfully deserted. *Probably a result of the closed border*, Shake thought as they dug him out from under the tarp. A multi-language sign in the parking area said they were 925 feet above sea level. Shake shook off a spell of vertigo and took several deep breaths. The air was fresh and cool after a couple of hours breathing fumes in the back of the minivan. He leaned against a nearby banyan, focused the binos and using his good arm, glassed the border checkpoint below their perch.

There were soldiers and border cops on both sides of the road that led through the pass across matching red and white barrier gates. The Thai guards looked better, more military, but not overly interested in their duties. And they really didn't have much to do. No traffic flow, just a few cars and some tourists aiming cameras and milling around what looked to Shake like three crumbling, whitewashed teepees isolated in a little clearing. If those were the famous three pagodas, they weren't overly impressive. Even Burma-obsessed Rudyard Kipling would have been hard pressed to wax very poetic about it.

The Burma side was a bit busier and a lot more confused. Border cops were waving their arms in efforts to turn a few vehicles around and deal with complaining tourists. The border was indeed closed at Three Pagodas Pass. He had no immediate idea what to do about that. He handed Pete the glasses and slid down onto his ass with a painful thump that nearly caused him to lose consciousness.

There was a long-winded conversation between Pete and Chesa. Shake was barely aware. He kept slipping in and out of a fog. And he was fighting hard to keep the chunk of water boo down. *With significant blood loss, you'll feel weakness, disorientation, nausea...*

Yeah, all of the above, and the wound was now sending stabs of pain through his system with every heartbeat. Antibiotics, some quick-clot and a blood transfusion would be the best fix, but that looked to be unavailable, at least until they reached some sort of hospital or emergency clinic. And the nearest one was over there across the border in Thailand.

Apparently, Pete and Chesa conversing in animated Burmese had come up with a plan of action. "The refugee camp is about a kilometer beyond the border crossing." Chesa knelt beside Shake. "Pete and I will drive down there and see what we can do about reaching it. If I can find my doctor friend, maybe we can borrow some medicines…" She mumbled off after that and Shake supposed that was because her plan didn't go much further, but he was in no shape to argue.

Pete helped him move to a patch of thick jungle beyond the overlook where he'd be out of sight in case some tourists showed up and started asking questions about a half-dead roundeye bleeding into the parking area. They left the shotgun and Endra with him and headed for the van. He heard doors slam and the engine growl as Pete steered out of the overlook and down the mountainside toward the border crossing.

Endra was behaving like a concerned Nanny, feeding him water and trying her best to make him comfortable. She didn't seem overly distressed about their situation, and if she still harbored thoughts about joining the valiant anti-government efforts in her native country, they weren't obvious. Endra cooed reassurances as if Shake could understand what she was saying. When he made motions to let her know he was OK and just wanting to rest, Endra wandered off a bit and sat fanning herself with a leaf she tore from a stand of elephant ears.

Shake hoped they could remain hidden and unmolested until Pete and Chesa returned from their reconnaissance. At fifteen, short and willowy like most Burmese females, Endra wasn't going to be much help as a crutch if they had to move in a hurry.

Pete parked the van near a shopfront in the little border town of Payathonsu. They planned to drop into a few places, ask questions, and feel out the situation along this section of the border. There was no question that the border was closed with more police and army presence than either of them could remember. Pete thought it was the KNP. The long border area where a number of shoot-outs with rebel factions had occurred in the past, made officials nervous. Chesa agreed, adding that the Tatmadaw ran agents into the camps in Thailand to identify refugees with ties to rebel groups. Whatever it was, the border was attracting serious official attention. Slipping across unnoticed with a wounded man barely able to walk was going to be difficult.

Pete's first stop was a little auto shop/junkyard on the outskirts where a friendly mechanic complained long and loud about the closed border. He was losing money from Thai customers who often brought their vehicles across on day-passes for cheap repairs. He said the border cops were looking for some people involved with a shooting up in Mae Sot. The mechanic had heard it was something to do with the KNP, but he had no details. The Tatmadaw was in the area now patrolling in the hills and the heat was on the Burma side.

Chesa discovered mostly the same sort of information when she wandered through some of the shops around the center of the town pretending to snap photos. She found a little pharmacy that had some helpful things, strong disinfectant and even some tetracycline tabs, but the prices were sky high, and she had only a little *kyat* that Pete had shared from the remainder of Shake's cash.

What she wanted was something penicillin-based like amoxicillin. She was becoming very concerned about Shake's wound. It was clearly becoming infected and that had to be treated before dirt, weather, jungle, and germs turned it to gangrene. She'd seen it before in the camps where refugees arrived with relatively minor wounds left untreated to become badly infected. Sometimes they could disinfect and sometimes the wounds were too rotted for immediate help. The result was too often permanent crippling or amputation.

They met at the van to confer about three hours later. Hiking across the border through the jungle-covered mountains on either side of the pass was a nonstarter with Tatmadaw patrols combing the area. And it didn't look like the regular crossing points were due to open any time soon. And even when they did, the mechanic told Pete, traffic was likely to be restricted to visitors in either direction that had valid day passes which could only be gotten—or purchased on the Burma side—from the Border Police. Simply driving across the border into Thailand appeared to be no option. Perhaps they'd be forced to call Walter and see if there was anything he could do—if he wasn't already dodging authorities in Thailand.

Chesa decided they needed to deal with first things first. And the first thing on her mind was obtaining medicine for Shake Davis. She returned with Pete to the little pharmacy where she identified herself as a nurse and asked about penicillin-based antibiotics. The wizened little man behind a counter admitted he had a small supply of amoxicillin on hand, but obtaining it would require a doctor's prescription.

"Suppose a man had no doctor…just a nurse…" Pete pointed at Chesa. "…surely there would be some accommodation that could be made."

The little proprietor leaned across the counter and whispered. "I do not deal in illegal drugs."

"Of course not." Pete leaned in closer. "Legal drugs only…and where to you get the legal drugs?"

The proprietor waved a hand. "From Thailand. There is a shop over there. We do business…when the border is open."

"So, if you were to sell some drugs…to a nurse…in order to save a man's life, that would be an act of charity and kindness."

"A very expensive act of charity and kindness…"

Pete and the chemist stared unblinking at each other until both understood the deal. Pete nodded and turned to leave. Chesa followed him out of the shop. "Where are we going?"

"To get enough money for an act of charity and kindness."

ဝဏ

Shake thought maybe the long, quiet rest in the shade of a gnarly old nipa palm might have restored some strength. He was slowly inching up to a sitting position to test that proposition when he heard Endra scream. On one hand and knees, he crawled toward her voice and a disturbance that sounded like a full-tilt wrestling match in the nearby bush. Favoring the wounded shoulder and nearly useless right arm, he thrashed his way to a little pool of mountain water that was verdant with pond scum. Near that water hole with her naked legs kicking and splashing, Endra was in a losing battle with a huge snake.

Shake shouted for her to lay still, remembering a documentary he'd seen on Burmese pythons being hunted in Florida. From what he could tell, this was a prime example, a thick-bodied serpent with muddy brown and green splotches. Shake considered crawling back to get Pete's shotgun, but the way the snake was coiled around Endra, he didn't see much chance for a shot that wouldn't also kill her. He jacked his leg up and reached for the five-inch Kershaw folding blade that he kept tucked in a boot top. It wasn't much against a snake that had to weigh upwards of 50 or 60 pounds, but it would have to do. Endra was gasping for breath as the python squeezed on her diaphragm. Her legs were pumping like pistons, but the snake's pulsing body had her arms tightly pinned.

Supported by only his good left arm, Shake scrambled toward the struggle and tried to ascertain where the python's head might be amid the tangle of girl and snake. Endra helped with that as she writhed, trying to shake loose. Near her left shoulder, he saw the spatulate head with forked tongue tasting the air and dark, beady eyes fixed on an approaching threat. Something Shake had seen or read made him think the head was the vulnerable part of a snake this large, but he could hardly expect the python to hold still while he drove a knife into it.

He reached for the snake with his weakened right hand, fighting a searing jolt of pain as blood began to flow from his shoulder wound. Ignoring that as best he could, Shake caught the big serpent's body just behind the head and rolled it away from Endra's body. It was like trying to muscle a high-pressure water hose. He could feel powerful muscles bulging and throbbing as the snake tried to escape his grasp, but Shake managed to pin a section of the python to the ground long enough to drive his knife into what he hoped was the snake's brain.

Maybe Burmese pythons didn't have brains. Or maybe he just missed it, but at that point things really got interesting. As Shake kept stabbing away with the Kershaw trying to do as much damage as possible, the snake shifted targets.

Whipping its thick body into the air, the python released its hold on Endra and began to curl around Shake. As he twisted to avoid the coils, Shake saw Endra leap to her feet and sprint away, her bare feet splashing muddy water. She was safe, but Shake was in trouble and getting weaker by the moment.

It felt like he was being locked into some sort of medieval torture device featuring iron bands that tightened in one direction each time Shake moved in another. And the more of the snake's coils that wrapped around his body, the harder it was to use his one good arm to keep stabbing. Shake gave up on the head and started to stab and slash at every scaly surface imprisoning his body. The snake didn't seem to mind all that much and just kept squeezing.

His vision was beginning to tunnel toward dark pinpoints as his breathing was more and more restricted by the python's muscular coils. Shake used his legs as leverage, trying to roll against the coils but it didn't help. The snake had most of its eight-foot length wrapped around Shake's body and the lights were about to extinguish when he heard the boom of a shotgun. He felt buckshot bite into his hip and thigh, but it was pinpricks against all the other pain he was feeling. The snake jerked with one final spasm and then lay still.

As Shake tried to push his way out from under the still python, he heard another shot so close he felt the heat from the muzzle blast. He looked up to see Endra with Pete's old double-barrel coach gun in hand. She'd nearly blown the python in half with the first shot. The second barrel ended the nearly fatal wrestling match and Endra began to drag the shredded carcass out of the arena. When she got Shake clear of dead snake, she dropped the shotgun and wrapped her arms around him, babbling in tearful Burmese.

ဘဏ

Pete and Chesa were struggling with laboring lungs and aching legs as they climbed the last part of their hike up to the overlook from Payathonsu. Pete struggled under the weight of Shake's rucksack and hobbled along as best he could on his prosthetic to keep up with Chesa's strides. They were too winded to continue discussing the wisdom of selling the beat-up old van. By the time they reached the mechanic's lot after leaving the pharmacy, they'd almost agreed that it was necessary. They were trapped in Burma without wheels, but they did manage to make the money stretch to cover some serious antibiotics and medical supplies that might save Shake Davis's life. And both agreed they wanted to do that whether they eventually reached Thailand or not.

The pair had stopped to catch their breath just below the overlook when they heard the first blast from a shotgun. That was followed by a second shot as they ran up the final stretch and entered the empty parking lot. Chesa heard her sister crying from somewhere in the surrounding bush and led the way crashing through the undergrowth and tangled vines toward the sound.

Endra spotted her sister and ran shouting and pointing. Pete took a quick look at the shredded snake and then knelt beside Shake who was barely conscious and covered in fresh blood. "Most of it's his…" Shake managed to mumble before he lost consciousness. Pete dropped the rucksack and dug around for bottled water that he used to wash Shake's face and shoulder.

"The snake had me…" Endra panted out her story as Chesa rushed to evaluate the man they had come to save. "Mister Davis wrestled with it and got me free, but he was

in trouble…only a knife and one arm…so I got the gun…"
Chesa hugged her sister and took a look at the dead serpent.
She seen a number of them, but this one was a monster. Prob-
ably waiting for some supper near the little pool and deciding
Endra would do. "I shot the snake…" Endra led the way to
Shake's prostrate form and pointed at a bloody patch on his
right hip and thigh. "…but I think I killed Mister Davis."

"You didn't kill anything but that snake." Chesa knelt to
examine the new wounds. She retrieved Shake's knife from
his hand and cut away a scorched section of his trousers.
Likely some shot embedded there but nothing life threatening, and Shake was still breathing regularly. "You saved this
man, Endra. Now we must see what we can do to keep him
alive."

๛

They made Shake as comfortable as possible flat on his back
with his head resting in Endra's lap. Chesa thought it a bless-
ing that the wounded man kept passing in and out of consciousness. She had some painful procedures to perform and
no anesthetic beyond some topical gel and a handful of mild
painkillers. She dosed her patient with the amoxicillin tabs
and sent Pete to retrieve the old sewing kit she'd found in
Shake's rucksack. It was the kind of thing a man accustomed
to rough repairs carried in the field and included large gauge
needles and a supply of waxed thread. When it came time to
suture the wound her efforts would likely leave an ugly scar.
From the look at the other scars, punctures, and puckers on
his torso as she stripped him down for surgery, it would be
nothing new for Shake Davis.

Chesa set Endra to work attempting to sterilize her makeshift instruments with a bottle of medicinal alcohol the

village pharmacist had thrown in with their purchases. Her first task was to debride the dead flesh from around the four-inch gash in Shake's deltoid muscle. Much of the flesh had putrefied to coarse ridges and that had to go so that she'd be sewing healthy flesh when she closed the wound. As she swabbed with Endra patting away fresh blood with a supply of surgical gauze squares, Shake's eyes popped open, and he glanced around trying to determine what was happening to him. Chesa fed him some of the painkillers with a big slug of water.

"I'm going to sew up this wound," she said in her best bedside voice. "But first I will have to cut away some dead flesh. You might feel some discomfort."

"If that damn snake didn't kill me, you probably won't either." Shake groaned and tried not to look at the surgical scissors Chesa was holding. "Just do what you've got to do…except amputate. Let's stop short of that if possible."

Pete straddled him, pinning Shake's good left arm under a knee, and nodded at Chesa to begin the debridement. As gently as possible, she began to snip away at the dead flesh around the wound. Shake did his best to just ride with the pain, remembering times on distant battlefields when he'd had to do something similar waiting for a Corpsman to arrive. When that happened, the Doc usually had some morphine to administer. This time he'd just have to bear whatever it took to get him sewed up against further blood loss and infection.

As Chesa worked, chatting with Pete and Endra in whispers, he ground his teeth against the pain and thought about wounded Marauders in these same jungles during World War II. Those rugged, rock-hard bastards probably endured similar ordeals as Medics probed and tried to treat Japanese bullet wounds. "Respect…" He whispered and then passed out.

When he flashed back into consciousness, he thought another python had arrived and was chewing on his shoulder. It was Endra pinching flesh together as Chesa deftly sewed up his wound with a large needle trailing a length of waxed thread. "Just a few more stitches," she said. "We've got the bleeding stopped."

"That mean I'm likely to survive?" His entire right shoulder and upper arm felt like someone had been pounding on them with a sledgehammer. But it was a dull ache rather than the piercing pain he'd felt before, so he called it an improvement.

"The prognosis is good," Chesa smiled at him. Pete was still sitting astride his torso, but he was wearing a big grin. "Missus Chesa do good job, Shek! You be OK."

Probably so. And whatever they'd dosed him with was already having some effect. The inflamed tentacles of infection he'd felt spreading across his chest were receding to just an irritating itch. "I guess you must have found your doctor friend."

"No. There was no way to get across the border…"

"We sell truck, Shek. Missus Chesa buy medicine."

"You sold the van?"

"Yes…we didn't have the money for the medicine you needed. Pete made a deal…and then we used the cash to buy antibiotics and a few other things to get you patched up."

"But how…"

Chesa waved off the question. "The border is closed and likely to remain that way for a while. The Army is patrolling in the hills. There was no way we could use the van to get us across into Thailand. So…" She shrugged, tied off the last in a long, jagged line of sutures across Shake's shoulder.

"That's the best I can do. I'm afraid you'll have another ugly scar to go with the others."

Pete uncoiled from his position and grinned. "Is ugly, Shek." He pointed at Endra and winked. "Woman like when man have this…"

"Yeah, Pete. Chicks dig scars." And then he passed out again.

ၵၵ

It was dark when Shake finally awoke and glanced around the little jungle clearing. Much of the brain fog had cleared and in moonlight that penetrated the overhead tree cover, he could see Pete curled up nearby being spooned by Chesa on one side and Endra on the other. His shoulder was still painful but bearable with the antibiotics and bush surgery efforts. Chesa had strapped his right arm to his chest with some spare webbing from his old rucksack, and as long as he didn't try to use that limb, the pain was bearable. But he was weak and unsure of his endurance.

His watch indicated it was just after three in the morning. A couple of hours until dawn and they needed to make a move—of one kind or another. The options were slim. Push comes to shove, they could always just turn themselves in to the Burmese border cops at the Three Pagodas Pass and hope for the best. He had his American passport and Chesa's had been returned to her, so they'd be OK after some inevitable lengthy hassle, and likely allowed to cross into Thailand. Pete and Endra would be another case. Endra had no papers of any kind, and that meant she'd likely be detained in some sort of Burmese holding pen for displaced persons. And very likely before her sister could do much about it, the teenager would find herself scooped up by human traffickers and sold off to some pimp. Elements of the Tatmadaw were notorious for that kind of thing. Pete had fixes in with the Border cops up in Myawaddy and was a well-known entity on both sides of the border in that area. But his involvement in the firefight and the KNP factor might change his status and land him in prison. Shake was determined to get all hands safely across the border, so surrendering them to an unknown fate at the hands of the Burmese authorities was not a viable option.

If he was healthier, if he was working with people who could move silently and avoid patrols, he'd take a shot at a night infiltration, but that didn't seem like a solid bet. He was in shit-shape, Chesa and Endra were strong but inexperienced, and Pete would have a hard time snooping and pooping through thick jungle mountains on just one good leg. There had to be another way.

He reached for the sat phone in his pocket. It was showing fair reception which Shake credited to the altitude of the mountain overlooking Three Pagodas Pass. It was also showing marginal power remaining and another slew of missed messages from Walt Ngo's number. He selected the most recent, punched replay and held the phone to his ear.

"Shake! Jesus Christ, man! Call me! They've closed the border all over here and…well, I heard what happened…Jesus, man…I'm sorry about that. Bad idea, I know. But I need to know if you and Chesa are OK. Just let me know where you are, OK? Just let me know…I'll work something out from here. Really, really sorry, man. But let me know where you are. Call me!"

Walter Ngo sounded either drunk or delirious with overtones of pure panic. Shake thought it over carefully. Could be the Thai authorities had somehow associated him with the shoot-out near Myawaddy so close to their border. Maybe he was under pressure on the Thai side for meddling in Burmese affairs. But that seemed unlikely. According to Chesa, the Thai authorities were accustomed to fleeing refugees from Burma, and they usually didn't raise much stink about it, assuming the Burmese authorities didn't press the issue or bring the violence across the border line. But the Thai attitude and authority didn't stretch across to the Burmese side.

Could be the KNP was over in Mae Sot looking for Walter Ngo's scalp as a result of the gold rip-off. But those clowns didn't appear to have that kind of international reach. And even if they hired local Thai hitters to settle a score with some roundeye it was a risky proposition likely to cost more money than the KNP could raise in a hurry.

An option would be to use the sat phone's remaining power and contact Ngo, let him know where they were and just sit right until he worked something out to buy or bribe their way across the border. Maybe, like a lot of other things he'd seen in the area, it was just a matter of putting the right amount of cash in the right hands. Surely, Walter Ngo and his frat-rat partner could do that even if they weren't worth a damn at anything else so far.

Or could they? If they had that kind of cash at hand, why try to pull off something like the fake-gold scam? Why not just take the hit? Why not just pony up the ransom and save your beloved wife no matter how much money it took out of your pocket? Unless you didn't really have that kind of money in your pocket in the first place.

Shake thought back on the meetings, events and discussions since the day Walter Ngo came to see him in Texas. He couldn't recall any talk of paying him to undertake the rescue mission. He'd been so emotionally wound up in the story and in his own grief over losing Chan that he'd never thought to ask about it. He remembered a conversation at the Irrawaddy Resort. Something about getting plenty of money once the mission was accomplished but nothing specific, no numbers involved. Had they been running this whole deal on spec? Was the single bar of gold and the cash for expenses along the way, all the money high rollers like Walter Ngo and Chris Anthony could raise? Was that why they tried to pull off the fake gold deal?

He heard the familiar sound of an aircraft climbing through the muggy air and spotted anti-collision lights flashing as the plane passed heading north. That gave him the glimmer of an idea. He dug around awkwardly in his pockets using just one hand to sort through the litter until he felt the crumpled card he wanted. Then he powered the phone and tapped out the digits written on the back of the card. He was beeped to a message service when he reached Chunky Cuthbert's private number in Rangoon.

"Chunky? It's Shake Davis, the Marine you flew up to Myawaddy last week. I'm in a bind. Gotta play the U.S. Marine payback card, mate. Call me, Chunky. I need a hand—badly." It was a last, long shot but something about the way the former RAF pilot talked about Marines and his combat experience made him hopeful.

At dawn, Pete meandered off into the jungle and came back with an armful of edible fruit. They chewed through a breakfast of pomelo, papaya, and jackfruit while Shake led a discussion of their options. Chesa translated for her sister who agreed at this point in her experience that throwing themselves on the mercy of the Burmese authorities was a bad idea. Pete thought waiting it out in the jungle for the border to reopen didn't have much merit. He'd seen troop carriers winding up the road from the AH-1 and thought the Tatmadaw was reinforcing the border.

"One time before…Karen and Mon try to take Three Pagoda. Much fight in this place. Tatmadaw maybe think KNP try again."

Shake nodded and shifted to ease the pressure on his shoulder. Likely the Burmese Army was knee-jerking over the gunfight at Myawaddy, presuming it had something to do with an offensive by the KNP or another of their dreaded Ethnic Armed Organizations. If his sat phone had enough juice left, he'd call Major Sherman Semple in Rangoon for an intel update, but it was red-lining and he had no way of recharging. He wasn't even sure there was enough life left in the battery to handle a return call from Chunky Cuthbert if that ever came.

He was pacing, trying to work some of the stiffness out of wobbly legs and an aching back when the phone vibrated against sore ribs. It was Chunky. *Thank you, God.*

"An unexpected pleasure, Shake! What's all this about a bind? Get caught diddling a native lass?"

"Chunky, I'm on a phone that's about to die here, so I've gotta make it quick. I need you to pick me up and get me across the border into Thailand. Can you do it?"

"Depends, mate. Jolly and I are picking up our Jet Ranger out of service this morning, so we've got the platform. Where are you?"

"Just above Three Pagodas Pass…on the Burma side. You know the place?"

"Sure. Big tourist attraction. But it's a long stretch for a Bell 505. Have to refuel between here and there. And then there's the business about flying into Thai airspace. Have to file a flight plan and the like…"

Shake could hear the phone beeping. He didn't have long to do much more than beg. "Chunky, I really need your help, man. I'll explain it when I can but please pick me up. It will be me and three pax. You can set down in a parking lot here…there's an overlook deal…"

The phone went dead.

Rangoon

E asy day, Jolly…and we've got to fly a test hop any- way. Stop nattering and let's get on with it." Chunky Cuthbert made a final tic on their preflight checklist and strapped into the left seat of their Bell 505 parked on the maintenance ramp.

Jolly Withers donned his headset and switched on master power. "Your standard test hop don't involve going all the way to Three Pagodas, picking up some dodgy pax and plunking them down over in Thailand…where we ain't sup- posed to fly, by the by…"

"Nothing dodgy about Shake Davis, mate. He's a Ma- rine. He needs help. That's good enough for me." They watched the ramp dog at the skids pull tie-downs and give them a thumbs-up to engage the rotors. Jolly screened the instrument displays and saw no mechanical or electrical rea- sons to dawdle. "The bosses might have another opinion, mate."

"This ain't a HeliUnion aircraft, Jolly."

"But we *are* HeliUnion pilots, mate. And I'd sort of like to keep that job for a while."

"The company needs us worse than we need them, mate. All present and correct. Let's pull pitch."

As the Bell Jet Ranger lifted and turned into the wind, Chunky cleared them for departure and Jolly punched coor- dinates for Three Pagodas Pass into the Inertial Nav System. They chopped up through some scudding clouds and hit an economical flight level. "What kind of bind do you reckon he's in…" Jolly stared down as the concrete sprawl of

Rangoon began to thin and verdant jungle began to appear below them.

"Don't know…" Chunky lit a cigarette and shrugged. "I'm hearing some rumors about troubles and rebel groups and a shoot-out near where we delivered our pax last week. Reckon it might have something to do with that. His phone died before I could get any details."

"I thought this man Davis was photographing the countryside. Something to do with a video game or somewhat."

"More likely somewhat, Jolly. I spoke with a Royal Marine mate after we dropped him off last week. Just curious, you know? My mate knew all about former Chief Warrant Officer Shake Davis. And he ain't the kind of duffer that shoots happy snaps for a videogame. Got more trigger time in hot spots around the world than you and me got stick time."

"Chunky, we ain't flyin' combat these days. Not sure I want to start that stuff again…"

"Once in, never out, mate. When the tangos shot me down over in the Sandbox, it was U.S. Marines that hauled my bleedin' arse out of big trouble. And then the buggers fought their way through a horde or two and carried me back to friendly territory. Hadn't been for those gents, I'd likely be dead or pissin' blood in some Taliban torture chamber."

Jolly worked the radios to arrange a refueling stop and then they flew in silence for a while. Jolly had never been shot down in combat, but he understood the sentiment Chunky was feeling. He had a lot of mates from his Commando days that he felt confident would do whatever was necessary if he needed help. It was the Band of Brothers thing. Not cliché. It was real.

"So, we pick up Davis and three pax somewhere near the overlook on the Burma side of Three Pagodas?"

"That's the plan."

"How do we find them?"

"Beats me, Jolly. I'm betting Shake Davis will find a way to signal or something. We'll just cruise low-level around the overlook area and keep an eye on the ground."

"And then we just saunter over the border into Thailand? We ain't filed or cleared for that, Chunky."

Chunky Cuthbert reached toward the nav system screen and tapped it with a flight-gloved index finger. "Dodgy system that, Jolly. Never can tell. It might just pack up and lead us astray."

Three Pagodas Pass

An eight-man Tatmadaw patrol was crapped out in the overlook parking lot around noon. Shake watched from the surrounding jungle with Pete prone by his side. Pete elbowed him and pointed at a patch on the pocket of a soldier's sweat-soaked fatigues. "Soldier from Myawaddy," he whispered.

"Shit…" Shake whispered back realizing the heat was still on and these guys were part of the border reinforcement. Murphy was definitely on the offensive. If something could go wrong on this jug-fuck of a mission, it would. He had no idea if Chunky Cuthbert would respond to his plea for help, but he had to believe an old soldier with a high opinion of the Marines would come through in the clutch. Given what he'd seen so far, it was about all he trusted.

Shake stared at the Tatmadaw troops in the clearing. He'd been on enough patrols to recognize when the soldiers involved were hot, tired, and pissed off. These guys were bound to park here for a while, guzzling canteen water, maybe even foraging around for fresh fruit. Why run when you can walk—and why walk when you can sit it out in the shade. They were smoking and joking much more than the corporal resting in a patch of nipa palm should allow, so he wasn't looking at disciplined and motivated troops. He *was* looking at a big problem if a forager found Chesa and Endra hiding back by the water hole. Or if Chunky—please God—showed up looking for a landing zone before it was clear of soldiers.

He needed a distraction, something to get these dudes up off their asses and back into the jungle. He needed this open area to be clear if and when Chunky and Jolly showed up overhead with an airborne Uber to fly them to safety across the border. These troops were supposed to be looking for trouble. Shake decided to give it to them. He nudged Pete and crawled away toward the little pool where the women were waiting.

"Soldiers in the overlook parking lot," he said when he was surrounded by his fellow fugitives. "We need to get them out of there and back into the jungle. I'm not gonna be much good for this, so it will be up to you all to provide a distraction." He dug around in his rucksack for a pack of three pencil flares. He'd been hoping to use them as a signal for Chunky's helicopter, but he'd have to scrub that. "Chesa, you take these flares down the mountainside to the north." He showed her how to load and fire the little projector. "Find a spot and wait. Pete, you take your shotgun gun down in the other direction to the south of the overlook. When you've got a spot deep in the bush, fire off both barrels. Chesa, when you hear that, pop the flares…high up into the sky. And then everyone beat feet back here. We'll rendezvous at the watering hole."

Endra said something to her sister and Chesa translated. "She wants to know what her job will be."

Shake smiled at the teenager. "Miss Endra, the fearless snake-killer, is gonna hold my hand back here and make sure I don't do something stupid." The translation caused Endra to giggle as she reached over to grab Shake's good hand. He gave her hand a squeeze and listened in silence as the others prepared to leave on their part of the mission. As he'd done so often in other jungles, he closed his eyes and listened intently, hoping to hear the familiar chop of rotor blades, but it was silent except for the occasional distant comment from the soldiers in the overlook parking lot.

Pete dropped a couple of buckshot rounds into his coach gun, snapped it shut, and stood to leave. Shake caught him by an elbow. "I hate ask you to do this, Pete." He tapped a knuckle on the driver's prosthetic. "You gonna be OK getting down and back up?"

"No sweat, Shek. Old soldier can do easy…even if only one good leg."

Shake gave his shoulder a tap. "Yeah, old soldier, and you use that one good leg to scramble back here on the double. You copy?"

"Copy all, Shek…" And Pete disappeared into the jungle heading south. Shake turned for a final word with Chesa, but she was gone. He saw the bush to the north swaying with her passage and checked his watch. Three hours since the abbreviated phone call with Chunky. Timing might be bad or it might be good, depending on way too many variables. He led Endra toward a spot in the jungle surrounding the overlook parking lot which he hoped would be clear of Tatmadaw troopers shortly.

ကဏ

There was more than a normal military presence at Myawaddy when Chunky and Jolly set the Jet Ranger down for refueling. A chatty, English-speaking mechanic at the commercial depot told them it was a pain in his ass as he had to spend most of the day in the hot sun refueling military vehicles. He also told them the build-up had something to do rebels, or guerillas, or something that had idiots in Yangon thinking there was an anti-government uprising at hand.

"What's odds our man Shake Davis has something to do with that?" Jolly Withers signed the fuel receipt and recovered their credit cards. "Photographer my old arse. That bloke's got CIA written all over him."

Chunky was busy with a roll of electrical tape on the tail boom and fuselage of their aircraft. "Could be, mate. Reckon he's got the chops for that kind of work." Chunky tore off a final strip of black tape and stepped back to admire his work. Registration number XY-3163 had become XY-8768. "Can't say it makes much difference, does it? I'm doing this for an American bootneck that needs help. That's all. End of chat."

Jolly shook his head and plopped into the Jet Ranger's right seat. "And you don't give a toss if that American bootneck is over here fomenting some sort of anti-government revolution?"

"Mate…" Chunky cinched into his seat and hit master power. "Shake Davis is good, but if the American spooks were serious about ousting those assholes in Rangoon, they'd need at least a hundred more of him."

The Jet Ranger lifted, hovered momentarily and then wheeled toward the south and Three Pagodas Pass.

ဘ

A half-hour later, scudding clouds drifted across the pass. Mister Murphy again, Shake thought as he polished the surface of the little mirror he'd pulled from his survival gear. With his pencil flares about to be expended as part of the distraction, he'd planned to catch the sun and signal Chunky with flashing light, but pale sunlight and looming cloud cover made that problematic. He was pondering alternatives when he heard the boom of Pete's shotgun off to the south in the jungle that covered the hillside. He shifted to look north and saw the first pencil flare arc into the sky.

The Tatmadaw corporal in charge of the patrol bolted upright and began to shout at his troops. He moved out into the murky sunlight and pointed as another pencil flare shot skyward. Troops were scrambling to collect their discarded gear when Pete fired a second shot from the jungle to the south. It was Keystone Kops in the overlook parking lot. Waving his arms and shouting at his groggy troops, the corporal divided them into four-man teams and sent them off looking in both directions. If the NCO had a radio, he didn't use it as he dithered for a few moments and then followed the team he'd sent north.

With the parking lot clear, Shake decided to hedge his bets by marking the LZ. What he needed was a back-up signal. A ground ID marker that would be visible from the air if he couldn't trap sunrays to reflect off his mirror. He grabbed Endra and led her out of the bush. Squatting in some loose dirt, he drew an X with his finger and pointed at the whitewashed rocks surrounding the parking lot. Endra seemed confused until she saw Shake struggling to pile the rocks into a pattern out in the middle of the parking area. She got the picture and scrambled to help.

He heard the first faint whop of rotor blades as he hustled back into the surrounding bush. It might be just another military or civilian bird beating the air overhead, but Shake had to believe it was Chunky and Jolly to their rescue. He cobbled together what gear he had left and tried to shoulder his ruck. Endra waved him off and strapped the pack to her own thin shoulders. Then she shouted something and pointed. Chesa, breathing hard and covered in dirt and sweat, barged into the little clearing. She looked upward and grinned. Through the tree cover, Shake saw a Jet Ranger swoop overhead and make a long, looping pedal turn, obviously eyeing the parking lot area. Chunky said they'd be flying a Jet Ranger, so it had to be him. But where was Pete?

ಎಲ

"Saw what looked like flares over about 11 o'clock…" Jolly waved a gloved hand toward the north side of the pass.

"Not our mob…" Chunky pulled a little pitch and kicked the helicopter around for another pass. "Bloke like Davis knows what we need to set down. He'd be in that parking area."

"Don't see anyone…" Jolly craned to peer out his side of the cockpit. "But there's an X laid out in rocks." Chunky kicked a rudder pedal and looked out to his side. "Yep…and X marks the spot. Going down for a closer look."

"Let's don't dawdle, mate. Looks like half the bloody Burmese Army is crawling around down by the pass."

ಎಲ

Shake stumbled out into the open waving his good arm overhead, watching as the Jet Ranger made a long, slow pass from north to south. Still no sign of Pete. He left Chesa and Endra by the X and told them to keep waving at the approaching helicopter. Then he limped into the bush on the south side of the clearing, yelling for Pete.

ಎಲ

"Two females down there waving at us." Jolly pulled off his sunglasses and squinted. "No sign of Davis."

"One of those birds is wearing his pack." Chunky nosed over to make another, slower pass. "Let's give it a minute."

"Can't afford much more than that, Chunky. I'm seeing military vehicles rolling in our direction."

 roa

Shake followed the sound of virulent curses when Pete finally responded to his call. The ex-soldier was about 30 meters below the parking area, hobbling on one leg and thrashing at entangling vines when Shake finally reached him. Pete had the coach gun in one hand and his prosthetic lower leg in the other.

"Sunnabeech! Sunnabeech leg tear off!" Pete showed his prosthetic which was wrapped in a snarl of liana vines. The straps that held it onto the stump of Pete's left leg were snapped and flapping.

"That helicopter is for us, Pete." He could hear Chunky maneuvering to set the bird down. There was no way he could carry Pete with his wounded shoulder. "We gotta go!"

"OK, Shek…" Pete reached into a cargo pocket and came up with a roll of tape. Shake grinned at Pete. Let no man enter a dicey spot lest he be armed with duct tape. "OK, Shek…you hold…I fix."

Shake propped Pete up against a tree and held the prosthetic in place while Pete wrapped his lower leg with about a mile of tape. It wasn't pretty but Pete stomped a couple of times and declared himself ready to go.

They broke cover in a blast of rotor wash as Chunky set it down right on the X. Jolly was shoving Chesa and Endra into the back as Chunky held the bird light on the skids. Pete clambered aboard and hauled Shake up after him. Jolly slammed the passenger access door and vaulted into his cockpit seat.

Chunky looked back wearing a devilish grin and twirled a finger. Shake shot him a thumbs up and the bottom fell out as the helicopter leaped into the air. Down below, Shake saw several Tatmadaw Land Rovers converge on the parking area. Lots of pointing fingers and wild gesticulation down there, even a few rifles pointed in their direction, but no one seemed willing to pull a trigger on a civilian aircraft. Chunky clawed for altitude and turned hard east, heading for Thailand.

Shake wriggled into a set of headphones and hit the transmit button. "Chunky…Jolly, you guys are lifesavers, literally!"

"Wait one, Shake…" Chunky checked his nav instruments and saw they were about to enter Thai airspace. He reached for the dash and flicked off the helicopter's transponder. "We are now an unidentified flying object. Don't want to stay that way too long, so where to?"

"We need to get back to Mae Sot, Chunky. You get us up there and it's end of mission."

"Just so we know how to duck and dodge…" Jolly craned over his seat to see the two female pax hugging each other and a grinning Burmese with one leg that looked like a badly wrapped tree stump. "…could you hit the highlights of that mission for us?"

"Call it a hostage rescue, Jolly. I know it probably looks like some cocked-up guerilla warfare stunt, but I was over here to deliver a ransom for these two." He pointed at Chesa and Endra. "They got taken by the KNP and the husband involved made a deal to pay with gold rather than cash. He's some kind of fat-cat videogame producer."

"Aha…hence the cover story about being a photographer on assignment."

"Yeah. My job was to set it all up, engineer the swap, and then get the women across the border. Almost went as planned until the husband pulled a scam. The promised gold turned out to be lead bars painted to look like gold. The KNP caught on at the last second and were not happy. Violence ensued, as they say, and the fucking Army got involved."

"That explains a thing or two…" Chunky began to fly nap of the earth heading north, hoping to stay below Thai air defense radar. "And likely resulted in that bunged up arm of yours."

"Yeah. Chesa's the wife. She's Burmese but American by marriage to the guy who cobbled this shit-show together. The other one is Endra, her younger sister. They did some butcher-shop surgery on a bad machete wound and saved my ass."

"Who's the one that looks like a duct tape test dummy?"

"That's Pete, my driver when we had a vehicle. He's former Tatmadaw, lost part of his leg to a landmine. We had to do some quick repairs when his prosthetic got ripped off in the jungle. Fuckin' guy's a magician with duct-tape."

"We're gonna have to make this a quick trip, Shake. Can't stay too long on this side of the line. You got any specific location in mind at Mae Sot?"

"Just set us down anywhere you can near the town, Chunky. I'll take it from there."

Mae Sot, Thailand

T hey landed in a weed-infested soccer pitch east of downtown Mae Sot. Shake dismounted and reached across to offer his left hand. "Wish I could find a way to repay you guys for the risk and expense. If I can raise some money…"

Chunky waved it off, shouting over the engine roar. "Debt's discharged, Shake…in a number of ways."

"Stay in touch, mate." Jolly said. "We might be looking for work Stateside before too long."

Shake grabbed a pen from Chunky's pocket and scribbled his contact information on the back of a checklist. "That's my address and number. You guys get to Texas, you've got a place to rack-out. Beer and barbecue are on me."

He led Chesa, Endra, and Pete out of the rotor wash as the two pilots lifted off, pausing in ground effect to make the Jet Ranger execute a polite little bow, and then zoomed off west toward Burma.

"Where is Walter?" Chesa sounded like she wanted to see her husband for a bit more than a reunion hug.

"I'm betting he's still holed up where he was when this all began…hotel called the Irrawaddy Resort."

Pete was sitting on a sideline bench re-wrapping his prosthetic. He tugged on the broken attachment straps. "Place near where I can get fix this."

Shake had been trying to come up with a plan for the encounter with Walter Ngo and Chris Anthony, but he needed more time to think. And get everyone cleaned up and rested. He eyed the coach gun in Pete's lap then picked it up and stuffed it in his pack. They needed a hotel room, and walking up to the desk with a shotgun dangling was unlikely to be met with enthusiasm. He dug around in his pack for a while and located his passport and the AmEx Platinum card he'd been issued in Bangkok. Assuming it was still valid, they wouldn't be cash strapped for a while.

"Here's what we do. We'll walk to a hotel, not the Irrawaddy but someplace nearby. Everybody gets cleaned up and Pete gets his prosthetic repaired."

"I want to see Walter!" Chesa had fire in her eyes. If he had to bet, he'd lay money that Walt Ngo was in for a quick and very expensive divorce. It would serve the bastard right, but he had a few other things to iron out with Waler Ngo before that train wreck took place.

"Chesa, let me talk to him first. Just a few minutes to get some things resolved and then he's all yours."

They got a pair of rooms at a quaint little place surrounded by tropical plants called the Picturebook Guest House. The woman at the desk had no problem with the credit card and her eyes lit up when the computer indicated it was a no-limit deal. As Pete started to hobble off toward town to get his prosthetic repaired, Shake caught him by an elbow.

"Once you get that thing fixed..." Shake pointed at Pete's leg. "Drop by the Irrawaddy resort. Nose around a little but don't let yourself be seen. I want to know if Walter and his buddy are still there."

While Chesa and Endra shared time in long, hot showers. Shake cleaned himself up as best he could and noted that his wound seemed to be healing. He was even able to maneuver his arm a bit to help him shave.

A little lobby shop offered expensive imported smokes and liquor. He bought a fat Cuban cigar plus a pint of Maker's Mark and retired to a little lanai. It was nearly time for a reckoning, and he wanted to do it right. His instincts screamed for action. Something like charging in on Walter Ngo and Chris Anthony and then beating the bulldog crap out of both of them. It wouldn't be hard. Even with just one good arm, and he could take Pete's coach gun along as a club.

He was trying to come up with an alternate and less bloody plan, immersed in cigar smoke, trying to bank the fire in his gut with bourbon, when Chesa arrived. She was lovely, freshly scrubbed, smelling of some tropical essence and dressed in one of the colorful tube-skirt and jacket outfits he'd seen in the hotel shop. She was carrying a bundle of bandages and tape as she sat next to him on one of the padded lounges and began to redress his wound.

"It looks much better," she said, smearing some sort of salve on the ridge of stitches. "But you'll need someone to remove my shoddy sutures in a week or so."

"Might just leave them in there." Shake sipped whiskey and smiled. "Give me something to remember you by."

"Unless you are not the man I believe you are, I don't think you'll forget much about this horrible experience."

"I've had a bunch of horrible experiences over a lifetime, Chesa…including losing my wife not too long ago."

Her expression melted a bit and she ran the back of a hand along his freshly shaved cheek. "I'm so sorry to hear that…" She taped gauze pads over his wound and patted it lightly. "I'm sure she was a lovely woman."

"Yeah…and long-suffering to put up with me. In a lot of ways, you remind me of her. She was half Thai. I loved her very much…" The whiskey was working, and Shake felt some of his tension ease. There was something so universally soothing in a woman's tender hands. Maybe your standard female human had an instinct for it, maybe it was genetic. Chan certainly had it. And so did Chesa Ngo.

"So…what will we do now?"

Shake puffed his cigar and fanned smoke away from Chesa's face. "A lot of that's up to you, Chesa. Have you got a plan?"

"Short term…" She shrugged and hugged her knees, "I need to get Endra refugee papers so she can return to the States with me. I want to get her into a good school. That may take a while but it's relatively easy. And I know people in the camps here who can help. And there's Walter. I don't know how to deal with him just yet."

"And long term?" Shake capped the whiskey bottle and flexed his shoulder. Painful and limited mobility but it would do for what he had in mind.

"I really don't know, Shake. A lot depends on what Walter has to say for himself. We have been married for almost ten years, and he's been good to me up until now. He paid for my nursing degree and spent a lot of money helping with the refugee situation over here…a lot of money he apparently couldn't really afford. It's hard for me to hate him despite what he did." She brushed locks of dark hair behind her ears. "On one hand, I'm very angry that he took such a stupid chance with my life and Endra's. On the other hand, I knew that he was having serious financial troubles, so there's a part of me that understands why he'd take such a risk. He had to do something, I guess. The alternative was leaving me to rot over in the jungle."

"Chesa, you're a smart person. And you've got guts. My feeling is that whatever you do, it will be the right thing for you and your sister. What worries me is you having what you need to survive. If he's broke…"

"Walter might be in money trouble, Shake, but I'm not. Over the years we've been married, I put away some money of my own. Walter doesn't know this, but I own a considerable amount of Lancer stock. And I have some other personal assets…" She let that linger behind an inscrutable smile.

"Guess I should have figured a woman like you would have a back-up plan. You don't seem like…"

"Like what, Shake? Like the typical Asian woman who lives in the shadow of her husband? Was your wife like that?"

"Not by a long, damn shot. I didn't mean…"

She laughed and pointed a finger at his nose. "I think you have a thing or two to learn about women, Shake Davis. Asian and otherwise."

"Guilty as charged. I lived too much of my life among men, often very hard men."

"Not men like Walter…"

"No, those kind of guys remain a mystery to me. I mean, what kind of man runs a serious bluff with his wife's life at risk? How can a guy stand to take that kind of chance?"

"They live in a much different world from yours, Shake. Love, honor, honesty…they mean different things to men like Walter and his crowd."

"But how can a good woman let herself love a man like that?"

Chesa shrugged and patted his knee. "Sometimes what a woman sees in a man is not what she gets. It's not that uncommon. And it works the other way around."

"People suck…"

"Some do…" She laughed and helped him into his shirt sleeve. "But most don't."

"Walter Ngo and his buddy Anthony do. I bought into their story hook, line, and sinker. Figured a corporate big shot had to be flush with cash, you know?"

"Walter is very good at running bluffs, Shake. That's a large part of how he got to be a corporate big shot."

"Well, as far as I'm concerned at this point, he's got a lot to answer for…to you and to me."

"Yes, indeed…" She stood and straightened her skirt. "So, who goes first?"

"Let me do it. I intend to take him to task for a few things I need to get off my chest."

They waited puttering around the hotel until dusk. Pete had returned stumping along happily on a repaired prosthetic to let Shake know his pals on the Irrawaddy Resort staff reported Walter Ngo was still in residence. Apparently, Chris Anthony had checked out earlier and hired a driver to take him to Bangkok. Shake sent Pete and Endra to supper on his hotel tab and walked with Chesa through town. If the Thai cops and military were excited about troubles across the border, they weren't making a big issue of it. The Friendship Bridges were still apparently closed, but the people of Mae Sot didn't seem overly upset by the situation. Commerce was pinched, but the pachinko parlors were roaring and the little clubs along the main drag seemed crowded.

At the resort, Shake stopped in the lounge area. "I know you want to get this over with, Chesa. So do I. But please just wait here for a little bit. Let me have my say and then I'll come get you."

Chesa pointed at the rucksack hanging from Shake's good shoulder. She knew the shotgun was inside it. "Promise me you won't shoot him?"

"It's tempting, believe me. But I took precautions against my temper. The gun's not loaded."

She stood tiptoe to give him a peck on the cheek. "It's OK…I need to brush up on my profanity anyway. Come get me when it's my turn."

There was a Do Not Disturb sign hanging from the doorknob to Walter Ngo's suite entry. Irrawaddy Resort had yet to catch up to western hotel technology and still had keyed locks on their suite doors. The one securing Walter Ngo's room was easy pickings for Shake and his CRKT multi-tool. He jimmied the lock and carefully slipped into a long dark foyer. He stood rock still, listening for sounds to indicate where Walt Ngo might be elsewhere in the suite. Nothing but crickets and geckos chirping in the bush that Shake remembered as being on the other side of a lanai attached to the suite's sitting room.

He quietly placed his ruck on the tiled floor and pulled out Pete's coach gun. It wasn't loaded but looked mighty damn intimidating. You could never tell about people, especially civilians in a state of panic. Could be that Walter Ngo was armed and primed to shoot anything he wasn't expecting to appear.

Shake slipped deeper, keeping his back to the wall. No sound, no TV or internet dings. As the sitting room came into view, he recognized some luggage and clothing he'd seen before, and there was an open laptop showing a Lancer Tech screensaver on the desk. Still no sign of Walter Ngo. Maybe he'd stepped out to eat, but the take-out food trash scattered around the room made that unlikely.

He peeked into a bedroom off the hall and saw Walter Ngo sprawled over a rumple of dirty bedding. There were three or four empty liquor bottles on the floor nearby. And the room reeked of stale alcohol and dirty laundry. Shake carefully checked the rest of the suite. Empty except for more liquor bottles and more take-out remains. The place was a mess, and apparently room service had been ordered to service elsewhere for the duration of Walter Ngo's stay.

He walked back to the bedroom and stood over the unconscious form. *So that's what a corporate high roller like Walter Ngo does when his shitty plans disassemble.* He gets hammered and stays that way until someone arrives to clean up his mess. Like a common no-guts drunk. But most common drunks didn't lay sprawled in an expensive suite in Thailand wearing designer skivvies.

Shake poked at Walt Ngo with the barrel of the little shotgun. "Rise and shine, asshole. We need to talk."

Ngo blinked a couple of times trying to see through the shadows and an alcoholic haze. His bloodshot eyes flashed between the double tubes of the coach gun and Shake's face as he scrunched into a protective crouch with his back to the headboard.

"Shake! Damn, man! I've been worried sick."

"More like you've been worried drunk." Shake cocked one hammer on Pete's coach gun and held it against Ngo's crotch. "I'm inclined to blow a hole in you and be done with it."

"No, wait a minute, Shake. Where's Chesa?"

"She and I managed to survive a major dust-up when your scam went sour. I got her out like I promised I would. She's nearby, but you probably don't want to see her right now. Chesa's likely to tear your balls off for that stunt you pulled."

"Listen, I can explain…"

"Well, you'd better get started, pal. And it better be good, because I've come to know your wife and she deserves a whole lot better than a scheming, slimy shitbird like you."

"It was Chris Anthony's idea…"

Shake cocked another hammer and shook his head. "Ain't gonna wash, Walter. You're the senior man. No matter who came up with this bright fucking idea, you're responsible."

"OK, look…I was in big trouble with my company. They were threatening to vote me out, and I didn't have enough stock or clout to prevent it. All my money was tied up, and I couldn't raise anything like a million in cash. Not in a hurry, not without the time it would take to liquidate some assets." Ngo swung his feet to the floor and started to stand. Shake used the barrel of the shotgun to push him back prone. "Take it easy, Shake. Look, I was in a bind. If I waited for cash, the KNP would likely kill her or sell her off, so we came up with this idea of running a bait and switch with the one bar of gold we could afford right away and faking the rest of it."

"And you recruited my dumb ass as the middleman? You talked me into the scheme, right after my own wife died, without letting me know it was all bullshit?"

"Shake, I was desperate…"

"You were also monumentally stupid, asshole! Did you stop to think that if your scheme failed, the first life at risk would be your wife's? You bet on long odds, Walter. Even a gambler like you should know how shaky it was."

"I figured with a guy like you fronting the deal we could pull it off."

"Well, you got that one thing right." Shake took a long, deep breath and lowered the hammers on the shotgun. "Out of respect for good women and loyal wives—yours and mine—I'm gonna forget that you nearly got me killed, Walter. But you're gonna pay…"

"Anything you want, Shake. I've got Chris Anthony down in Bangkok right now raising money and liquidating assets. We'll be flush in a week or two. Whatever you want…"

Shake bounced the shotgun barrels off Walt Ngo's head and shut him up quickly. "Here's what you're gonna do, shit-head. You're gonna call American Express and see that the card you guys gave me in Bangkok stays good until I say otherwise—and no limits. Let's take care of that right now." Shake pulled Ngo off the bed and led him toward the sitting area. He plucked the AmEx card from a pocket and flipped it down near the phones on the desk. "Get on the phone. The number's on the back of the card."

While Walter Ngo punched his way through the AmEx International phone tree, Shake found a bottle of Sailor Jerry's Jamaican rum and hit it. He wanted Ngo to think he was drunk and desperate when he made his next demands. It didn't take long, once Ngo reached someone at credit card services and read them the number on the card. They were used to working with big money customers and clearly Walt Ngo was one of them.

"All done…" Ngo hung up and eyed the rum bottle in Shake's hand. "You're cleared to use the card for anything you want anywhere…"

"I'm gonna believe you won't welch on that, Walter. It will go very badly with you if I get any kind of hassle using the card. I know some people in the American press that would cream themselves if I was to tell them about the shit you tried to pull over here."

"I'm good for it, Shake. Swear to God, man. I'll cover the tab."

"You better, asshole, and it's gonna be stiff." Shake hit the rum again and handed it to Walter Ngo. "Get a taste and stand by to copy." When Ngo swallowed a mouthful, he seemed steadier. "Now, I'm gonna use that card to get me to

Bangkok where I intend to buy Pete a brand-new Land Rover with deluxe options. You'll cover that…and you'll call Chris Anthony down there. Let him know he's gonna provide me a little pocket change. About a grand in green ought to get it. I never want to see that bastard again, so tell him I want it left in my name at the front desk of Lancer Tech headquarters. Get back on the phone."

Walter Ngo took another hit of the rum and punched a preset number on his mobile phone. Anthony asked for some details, but Ngo shut him up quickly when Shake pointed the shotgun at him. The cash would be waiting in Bangkok.

"Just so you can track expenses on your card, Walter, be advised I'm gonna spend my time and your money for a couple of days in Bangkok. If it's pricey, I'm gonna do it. And then you're gonna buy me a first-class ticket back Stateside. Is all that clear?"

"It's clear. You won't have any problems."

"I'd better not, Walt. Now for the last thing. Just because I'm gone, you aren't off the hook. You're gonna use whatever juice you've got left to help Chesa get her sister some refugee papers and a trip back to the States when Chesa goes. I'll be watching, and Chesa is gonna be reporting to me. If there's any cockups, slick financial moves, or glitches in all that, I'll come looking for you, Walt. And you will not survive that encounter."

Shake left Walter Ngo with the rest of the rum, retrieved his rucksack and went out to meet Chesa in the lounge. "Your turn," he said.

"How is he?"

"About half-drunk. Looks like he's been that way for a couple of days. Crying the poor ass and feeling sorry for himself."

"I'd expect that…"

"Yeah, and somewhere inside I suppose he really is sorry. Because his scheme fell though or because he put us in serious danger? I don't know. Maybe you will. He's in Suite 104."

Chesa nodded and stood to leave. Shake draped an arm over her shoulders. "I made some demands that are gonna cost him some serious money, but he says his pal Chris Anthony is already raising cash for him down in Bangkok. He's apparently selling most of what he owns to make good on everything. I believe that. But you keep an eye on things for me." Shake handed over a sheet of hotel stationery. "There's my Stateside phone and email. Stay in regular contact. Let me know if you smell anything but Walter's dirty laundry…and don't let him pull any more cons."

"Are you heading home?"

"Shortly. First I've got to buy a new truck for Pete and throw him a little party down in Bangkok."

Chesa reached up to pull him down for a kiss. "Thank you for everything. You're a good man, Shake Davis."

"Damn, I hope so. Tell Endra the snake killer that I want to see her first report card."

ဘ

Shake and Pete bought some new clothes and rode a bus down to Bangkok. They checked in to the Mandarin Hotel where the concierge found them an address for a Land Rover dealer. It took a full day to find the vehicle Pete wanted. It was a metallic green Defender with all available bells and whistles and ready to roll off the showroom floor. Shake plunked down Walt Ngo's AmEx while Pete signed the necessary paperwork. It took another day for the credit card purchase to be approved, but they wasted no time waiting for that. When Shake dropped by Lancer Tech headquarters, the money was waiting for him, and he gave it all to Pete who instantly wanted to embark on an epic Bangkok pub crawl. Shake readily agreed to the proposition but insisted that Pete keep the cash. The meals and drinks were on Walter Ngo.

Also on Ngo's AmEx tab was a new iPhone and a laptop that Shake bought for Pete in a more sober moment. He wanted to be sure Pete could stay in touch and keep an eye on Chesa and Endra back in Mae Sot. He wanted regular reports from multiple sources, and Pete would provide good intel once he learned how to use the computer.

Three days later, Pete drove Shake to the airport in his brand-new vehicle. They were stupendously hungover, and Pete spent the time in traffic jams fiddling with all the new buttons, cameras, and amenities in his frigidly airconditioned new ride. Pete lost no time overriding the new car smell with smoke from his hand-rolls. Shake had seen a lot of happy people in his time, but Pete had them all beat hands down. At the airport, Shake pulled a trinket from his pocket, something he'd bought at a little shop during their tour of the nightspots. It was an intricately carved jade Buddha on a gold chain. Before he climbed out to catch his flight, Shake hung it over the rearview mirror.

"That's for you, my friend. Something to keep all your Nats in line."

Pete jammed the vehicle in park—he'd insisted on an automatic transmission to favor his pedal control—and hugged Shake. There was a flood of tearful Burmese but Shake ignored it. He caught "Good soldier, Shek…good man…good friend. Thank you…thank you for everything." It was all he needed to hear.

Lockhart, Texas

O ne of the gusty wind and rainstorms that Texans call blue northers was blowing over the little town as Shake Davis sat on his screened back porch scrolling through emails. He chuckled at Pete's first fractured English email experiments. Apparently, he had been keeping close tabs on the sunnabeech Mr. Ngo and helping Endra with her refugee paperwork. Pete started an enterprising shuttle service ferrying tourists back and forth from Burma to Thailand after the Ngo family left for the States. That was going fine.

Shake was distracted by a thumping somewhere down near his feet. It was the little puppy that he'd picked up at the local pound just after getting home when he found the silence in the big house too hard to handle alone. He thought nothing could ever replace Bear, but this little female pup was doing her best to change his mind. She was a cute little lab mix with a great personality. Her default mode was to sit and tilt her head if she didn't understand what was needed or wanted by her human friend. She'd done that at the pound and promptly captured Shake's heart. He named her Champagne Molly for her light blonde coloring and just because he had always like that old Leon Redbone tune. Shake scrubbed a spot behind her ears and was repaid by a wet nuzzle from Molly's nose.

He brought up Chesa Ngo's latest email. Apparently, her husband—she didn't know how much longer he'd be able to claim that tax exemption—had managed to liquidate enough personal property to get a huge stack of overdue bills paid and get them all out of Southeast Asia. Chesa and her sister were back in Las Vegas where Shake had hooked them up with Mike Stokey and his wife Linda. Chesa had her Nevada nursing credentials and was working in one of the area's better hospitals. Endra was a genuine green card resident alien and intending to apply for American citizenship when she finished high school.

Shake pulled the AmEx Platinum card out of his pocket and studied it. The little plastic banker had greased through the purchase of Pete's new Land Rover, a very pleasant flight home, and a bunch of other wild expenditures he'd made just to test Walt Ngo's sincerity. Never a hiccup along the way.

Shake closed his email program and stared at Chan's picture that he used as a screensaver. She was smiling with her arms wrapped around Bear, who was showing his customary goofy grin. God, how he missed them. He unwrapped a cigar, put his feet up on the butcherblock table, and flipped open his treasured book of Rudyard Kipling's poems. His gaze fell on an underscored line.

"For the temple bells are callin' and it's there that I would be. By the old Moulmein Pagoda, looking lazy at the sea. On the road to Mandalay..."

Thanks...but no thanks, Rudyard. Been there and done that. And then he torched the platinum card and used it to light his cigar.

About the Author

Dale Dye is a Marine officer who rose through the ranks to retire as a Captain after 21 years of service in war and peace. He is a distinguished graduate of Missouri Military Academy who enlisted in the United States Marine Corps shortly after graduation. Sent to war in Southeast Asia, he served in Vietnam in 1965 and 1967 through 1970, surviving 31 major combat operations.

Appointed a Warrant Officer in 1976, he later converted his commission and was a Captain when he deployed to Beirut, Lebanon with the Multinational Force in 1982-83. He served in a variety of assignments around the world and along the way attained a degree in English Literature from the University of Maryland. Following retirement from active duty in 1984, he spent time in Central America, reporting and training troops for guerrilla warfare in El Salvador, Honduras, and Costa Rica.

Upset with Hollywood's treatment of the American military, he went to Hollywood and established Warriors Inc., the preeminent military training and advisory service to the entertainment industry. He has worked on more than 50 movies and TV shows including several Academy Award and Emmy winning productions. He is a novelist, actor, director, and show-business innovator who now lives happily in Lockhart, Texas with Julia and Molly—spouse and dog respectively. He keeps trying unsuccessfully to retire.

Gunner Shake Davis, U.S. Marine Corps, might be out of the active ranks, but he's anything but retired. Catch all his adventures by bestselling author Dale Dye in the Shake Davis series of scintillating novels.

And catch Shake's daughter Tracey in her own action-filled adventure in Sea Hunt—available wherever fine books are sold.

For these and other quality military fiction and nonfiction, visit
www.warriorspublishing.com

www.ingramcontent.com/pod-product-compliance
Lightning Source LLC
Chambersburg PA
CBHW070635170726
48291CB00003B/1030